THE WALLFLOWER

FRANCES REYNOLDS

Quills & Quartos
PUBLISHING

Edited by Julie Cooper and Mary McLaughlin

Cover by Hoja Design

ISBN 978-1-956613-79-7 (ebook) and 978-1-956613-80-3 (paperback)

For my grandmother, the 'original' Frances Reynolds. I wish you could have been here for this.

CONTENTS

Prologue	1
Chapter 1	5
Chapter 2	13
Chapter 3	19
Chapter 4	23
Chapter 5	29
Chapter 6	35
Chapter 7	43
Chapter 8	47
Chapter 9	49
Chapter 10	53
Chapter 11	57
Chapter 12	63
Chapter 13	69
Chapter 14	75
Chapter 15	79
Chapter 16	87
Chapter 17	95
Chapter 18	101
Chapter 19	107
Chapter 20	113
Chapter 21	117
Chapter 22	119
Chapter 23	121
Chapter 24	127
Chapter 25	131

Acknowledgments   137

About the Author   139

Also by Frances Reynolds   141

SHIPBUILDING SCANDAL
March 17, 1811

Readers will recall the tragic sinking of *HMS Moyne* in a minor squall during her maiden voyage in January, with all hands lost. We have now learnt that the Surveyor of the Navy has uncovered despicable acts by the builder of the *Moyne*, Harper and Sons of Medway, which are likely the cause of the tragedy.

Two ships under construction for the Crown at the Harper shipyard were found to include inferior cuts of wood and 'devil bolts'—wooden pegs disguised as good nails by the addition of iron or copper caps to the ends. One other Harper ship remains afloat in the Channel, and will be brought to port with all speed for a thorough inspection. The Navy has severed its contracts with Harper and Sons on grounds of malfeasance, and the solicitors at Weems and Norton, London, have offered to represent the families of those lost on the *Moyne* in a suit against the shipbuilder.

WICKED WARSHIP-MONGERS
May 23, 1811

The scandal that emerged from the Medway shipyard of Harper and Sons after the loss of *HMS Moyne* has ignited like a barrel of gunpowder, engulfing several other firms engaged to augment His Majesty's Navy. The Surveyor of the Navy, having identified the culprit in the loss of 257 hands aboard the *Moyne*, then undertook to conduct unannounced inspections at dozens of other shipyards simultaneously. These were launched on the 1st of May, and we at the Post have been reliably informed that evidence of tactics similar to those of Harper and Sons, which line the pockets of the shipbuilder with Naval funds while risking the safety of our brave sailors, were found at a number of yards, among them such well-known concerns as Jones Brothers (Lyme), Walthorp Co. (Hull), and Jemison Yard (London).

Will the owners of these establishments flee to the former colonies, as Mr Harper and his sons are believed to have done? It is the opinion of this poor scribbler that they ought to end in gaol.

PATRIOTISM PREVAILS
June 11, 1811

At last, a bit of good news from a place that lately has seemed mired in treachery and corruption—the merchant shipyards of England. Specifically, the Thames-side yard of The Gardiner Company, long known as a preferred shipbuilder to the East India Company.

Having undertaken since the Year One to provide the Navy with a ninety-gun 'second-rate' ship of the line every three years, the yard was subject to the Surveyor's surprise inspection, mentioned in previous columns. There they found no cheap tricks, no inferior materials or shoddy construction, but a fine vessel only a few months away from joining her three sisters in the long battle against the Tyrant across the Channel.

You may wonder, readers, why this is newsworthy, for a number of other yards were found innocent of the corruption evidenced by the cowardly Harper and his ilk. The reason is this: The Gardiner Company has not only built quality ships for our good sailors, but has from the inception of the contract accepted payment for her Navy ships at a rate 7% less than they would require of the Company for similar vessels. Several employees of The Gardiner Company stated that the discount was instituted by the late Mr Neville Gardiner, founder of the yard, and continued by his nephew Mr Edward Gardiner, the present owner, out of nothing more nor less than love of King and country.

Let us all raise a glass, or a teacup, to that excellent brand of patriotism which quietly benefits our empire and the great struggle in which it is engaged, and restores to us our faith in mankind.

BARONETCY BESTOWED
August 2, 1811

Mr Edward Gardiner of The Gardiner Company, the shipbuilder justly lauded throughout England, is now Sir

Edward Gardiner, baronet, by decree of His Majesty. A statement from St James reads, in part, "Such loyalty and goodwill to the Crown and her Navy, conducted with no expectation of reward, has rightfully earned the admiration of Their Majesties, who anticipate receiving Sir Edward soon and expressing their gratitude directly."

As we await the trials of Misters Jones, Walthorp, and Jemison for their treacherous, one might even say treasonous, actions, let us also rejoice in the elevation of this most superior example of the English merchant class.

CHAPTER 1

ELIZABETH BENNET

I know Jane was as relieved as I was when my uncle's carriage lurched into motion, carrying us away from our father's estate, Longbourn. Uncle Gardiner looked on us with a knowing smile.

"Though I never thought you would accede to Mama's pleas," I said gratefully, "I must thank you for standing firm."

Uncle's eyes flicked heavenward. "There was never any question of Lydia joining you. As I told your mother, even were she old enough to be out in London, her manners are far from acceptable for the society there. The opportunities available for you in the circles I now have access to are too great, and too precious, to risk even having Lydia in my home when you and your aunt receive callers."

"I would say that fifteen is too young to be out even in Meryton," I grumbled. "In London—" I could not restrain a shudder "—she would not be satisfied until she had exposed herself and our entire family to ridicule."

"Even without Lydia, it is likely my popularity will fade as quickly as it came, and I mean to broaden your acquaintance while I may. Your mother and I agree: we should both like to see you well-settled and there is no one near Meryton worthy of either of you."

"And so we are to London and if at least one of us does not return home betrothed, we shall never hear the end of it," I laughed. "It will be up to you, Jane. We must find you a duke!"

Jane and my uncle laughed, and he shook his head. "I do not move in the very highest circles, girls, though I occasionally brush up against them now. Jane may have to make do with a baron."

"I should be quite satisfied with a gentleman who is honourable and kind, and able to support a family," Jane said softly. "It is very kind of you both to suggest that I could attract a great man, however." Though she is quite the prettiest girl in all Hertfordshire, my sister's beauty is exceeded by her modesty, and it is left to me to expect the best for her.

"I think you will also be well-received, Lizzy," my uncle said. "You will meet a greater variety of people than Meryton can boast, and some of those will value your wit and intelligence. You will surely make many friends and dazzle more than one gentleman."

My modesty is not so great as my sister's; I know I am a pretty girl, though not her equal. And yet, I did not share my uncle's optimism. "I shall hope you are correct," I replied, "though I am in no great hurry to marry. I wish primarily to have interesting experiences with interesting people. If I should happen to find love I shall not let it pass by, but I do not expect it."

"Whyever not, Lizzy?" my sister wondered. "Any man would be fortunate to earn your esteem."

"Because I believe that most young men prefer a certain docility in a wife, of which I am incapable. They may enjoy my company and flirt with me, but in the end they will choose a lady who defers to them in nearly everything. Since I had rather not spend a lifetime pretending to be someone I am not, I shall end a spinster and teach your daughters to be impertinent and neglect their lessons."

Dear Jane looked rather worried at that, but my uncle grinned. "Allow me," he said, "the distinction of under-standing my own sex better than a girl from a small village could, and accept my assurance that many men prefer a spirited wife. Jane will certainly have her admir-ers, but so shall you, and since you are so different, they are unlikely to be the same men, which will keep you from quarrelling over them." He paused as Jane and I laughed over the very notion, then added, "But for all your mother's exhortations, I hope you do not think of this time as a husband-hunting expedition. Enjoy your-selves in London, and meet new people. Some of them, no doubt, shall be young men, and if you form a worthy attachment no one will be better pleased than your aunt and me. But if you do not, no one will be disappointed, either."

"Except Mama," I retorted.

"In that case, I shall take the blame," he answered comfortably. "I shall tell her none of your suitors were worthy of you, and I drove them off."

We laughed again, and the talk moved on to other subjects. We three are well-suited to travelling together, and in amiable conversation the few hours of our journey flew by. Soon we were surrounded by the comfort and elegance of my uncle's home on Gracechurch Street, in the company of our excellent aunt, who has long been as a second mother to us—and, in my opinion, the better of the two. We had not seen each other since the Christmas season nine months gone, for my uncle's business and his elevation to a baronetcy had kept him tied to the city, so there was a great deal of news to share on both sides, and much happiness to be had in each other's company.

Beginning the very next morning, my aunt escorted us through a bewildering array of warehouses, linen-drapers, and milliners, ending in several hours with her own modiste. She was determined that we should suffer not a moment's mortification for lack of a fashionable wardrobe, and though we protested the expense, she would not be moved.

A music master was brought in to polish my skills at the pianoforte and to work with both of us on our singing, for it was certain we should be pressed to perform at some time or another. Fortunately, we both spoke French well and Italian passably, and were fully educated in comportment and dancing. Neither of us had ever claimed drawing or painting amongst our accomplishments, which my aunt rather lamented, but as we were both adept with stitchery, beadwork, and netting, she declared that we would not suffer by comparison with the ladies of society. Many of those, she confided, had no more claim to real accomplishment than moderate ability at the pianoforte, excellence in the dance, and a fair grasp of French, for all their 'superior' educations.

As soon as our new gowns began to arrive, our exposure to London's higher spheres commenced. Our first engagement was a dinner party at the home of Sir James Whitley, a baronet of some means and wide acquaintance. Nearly fifty people mingled in his spacious drawing room before the meal, and it was soon apparent that my uncle was the guest of honour. Everyone wished to make his acquaintance, and in so doing they also met his wife and nieces.

My head was swimming with names and faces by the time a handsome young man approached, hand outstretched to my uncle. "Sir Edward," he said, with the sort of broad, easy smile some call infectious. "I expect you will not remember me, but you and your uncle did some business with my father, Mr Joseph Bingley."

Uncle Gardiner positively beamed and warmly returned the clasp of hands. "Of course, of course—old Bingley was forever going on about 'my son Charles' this and 'my dear boy' that. May I say how grieved I was to hear of his death? A great loss to all who knew him."

"Thank you, sir. He is much missed. May I be made known to your companions?" He favoured us all with a genial smile, which brightened perceptibly when he got a good look at Jane.

The introductions were performed just in time for dinner to be announced. Mr Bingley escorted both Jane and me into dinner, though to his visible disappointment his own place was far from ours. I had my uncle to one side and a most pleasant young man to my other. He, it transpired, was in town to attend to some business related to his upcoming wedding. Our conversation centred upon books and gave me numerous new titles to seek out.

When the ladies withdrew, Jane and I were introduced to several young ladies we had not met earlier. One of them was entirely too willing to ask probing questions about our family, and the rest were insipid. Jane, saintly creature that she is, found them all quite pleasing.

As the gentlemen joined us, our little party thankfully broke apart, our new acquaintances removing to the sides of various gentlemen, though whether these were brothers, beaux, or prey, I could not determine. Mr Bingley was quick to find us and engage us both in conversation. His interest in Jane was entirely obvious, but he was far too polite to exclude me from the conversation. When I spoke he showed no impatience, unlike many a previous fellow enraptured by my sister's beauty. The Gardiners were in great demand, but still they found us several times in the course of the evening to assure themselves of our wellbeing.

Naturally, I could not but tease Jane over her admirer

on the return to Gracechurch Street, raising her blushes and laughing protests that she had known him for mere hours. She did concede that on short acquaintance he appeared to be everything a young man ought to be: sensible, good-humoured, and lively.

"His father was much the same," my uncle rumbled sleepily. "A most excellent fellow. I give you leave to like the son, Jane—you have liked many a stupider person."

Aunt Gardiner chided her husband for that jest, though it was apparent even in the dim compartment of the carriage that she, too, was amused by it. I laughed, of course, and even Jane chuckled and admitted that it was not untrue.

"I expect we shall see him again soon," he remarked after accepting my aunt's admonition in good humour. "For he asked our direction and stated an intention of calling."

Mr Bingley appeared in Gracechurch Street with admirable promptness, allowing only a day to lapse between the initiation of our acquaintance and the continuation of it. He was all smiles and amiability, and the bulk of his attention was still reserved for Jane. He repeated his visit both of the next two days, and struck me as rather puppyish—winsome and eager. My aunt and I were united in the opinion that if there was some backbone beneath that genial exterior he might prove a good match for my sister, who was too trusting and complying to be put into the care of a man who could not be firm when the occasion demanded it. We resolved to watch the development of their acquaintance with both hope and caution, and in the whirl of parties and balls over the next weeks, we saw little to alarm us.

CHAPTER 2

FITZWILLIAM DARCY

Before I had so much as set foot within Lord Alvanley's home, I deeply regretted having agreed to attend his ball. Alvanley himself was unobjectionable, though I was certain to be pressed into dancing a set with whichever of his seemingly endless stream of daughters was out at that moment. I do not generally care for balls, but resolved upon accepting the invitation that my friend Bingley might introduce me to Sir Edward Gardiner, whose ship-yard seemed a likely investment. One cannot always rely upon the whims of the land to provide for the future of one's estate and family, and Alvanley's ball had one other point in its favour: I was certain to find my uncle in the card room, and his company is ever a pleasure. No, the event itself was not the reason for my regret. That sat across the carriage from me.

"Dear Mr Darcy," purred Miss Caroline Bingley. "I do hope we shall have the pleasure of seeing you dance tonight. Such skill in the art as you possess ought to be displayed."

I glanced at my good friend, her brother, Charles Bingley. He looked apologetic, as he often does when we three are together. A gentleman does not visibly shudder when confronted with an avaricious female, so I held myself rigid and attempted to fend her off with words.

"It is unlikely that I shall dance more than my duty to my host requires. I had meant to decline the invitation altogether, but your brother informed me that it would be my chance to meet Sir Edward Gardiner."

"I had not thought you interested in such persons," she replied, surprised. "While it is true that he is all the rage at present, he is a tradesman, and no doubt shall be largely forgot in a twelvemonth."

"I am interested in the potential for a good invest-ment. Even when society no longer welcomes him, his business is likely to remain as stable and prosperous as it has been these past years. Forgive me for speaking of business matters, but you might be surprised how much is conducted even at the most exclusive events."

"I am certain you will like Sir Edward, Darcy," my friend interjected. "He is a gentlemanly, educated fellow, and his family are charming. Lady Gardiner is elegant and amiable, and his nieces delightful."

"Yes, Charles, we have all heard your rhapsodies on Miss Bennet," drawled his sister, rolling her eyes in a rather common fashion. "And next month you shall wax poetic over some other lady entirely, I am sure."

Bingley had the grace to look rather abashed, but insisted that though his attention had often been caught by a pretty face and pleasing figure, he had never before met a lady of such sweetness, or whose opinions coincided so perfectly with his own. I was not concerned; all of the ladies who captured his heart were unique to him until they were not, and then they were swiftly forgotten. Sir Edward's niece would surely be no different.

We were fortunate enough to encounter Sir Edward almost as soon as we entered the house, though not before Alvanley secured me for his daughter's fifth set. Bingley performed the introductions to Sir Edward, Lady Gardiner, and the Miss Bennets. I paid little attention to the ladies beyond the necessary civilities, for I was most interested in the new darling of London Society. Even the Prince Regent was said to be an admirer of Sir Edward's, which gave the man a certain cachet above even that which his patriotic actions and new title granted. He was well-dressed, well-spoken, and not at all coarse in his manner, at least during the few minutes of our initial meeting. Doing business with him would be no hardship at all, if this was how he continued to present himself. I secured his agreement to meet the following week, and was fortunate enough to be able to slip away while Miss Bingley was engaged in conversation with the man's nieces, no doubt at her brother's insistence.

I roamed the edges of the ballroom as I awaited my duty set with my host's daughter, speaking with acquaintances when I chanced upon them and ensuring that Miss

Bingley could not corner me. She was always prone to follow me through whatever company we shared, and as it appeared she had little acquaintance there, she had even less to distract her from her quest that evening. I had no desire to be seen with her on my arm—she had a regrettable tendency to claim it when I had not offered—thus it was important that I maintain an awareness of her whereabouts at all times.

By chance, I found a happy situation not far from the chairs set out for the chaperons and those ladies in want of a partner, where I was able to observe the company while largely screened by a tall plant. I remained there with my own thoughts, which primarily consisted of brooding over my young sister's near ruin at the hands of a fortune hunter two months previous, through the first two sets and half of the third before Bingley sought me out there.

"Come, Darcy!" said he ebulliently. "I must have you dance. I hate to see you standing about in this stupid manner. You had much better dance."

I denied any interest in the activity, citing a lack of ladies with whom I was well-acquainted. He chided me for not wishing to dance with any and every lady present, claiming an unusual bounty of pretty girls. I complimented the beauty of his own partner for the set, his Miss Bennet, but could not be drawn to allow that any other lady in the room was worth my efforts. He was happy to speak on her perfections for a moment, but then insisted that I must dance with her sister, who was, he said, sitting nearby. I recalled little of the girl save that she was as dark as her beautiful sister was fair, and made it abundantly clear to my friend that she had not impressed me and I would not be requesting her hand for a set. At last, Bingley accepted my wishes and left me in peace. Catching sight of an old friend from Cambridge, I abandoned my refuge and moved to greet him.

CHAPTER 3

ELIZABETH BENNET

"She is tolerable, but not handsome enough to tempt me. I am in no humour at present to give consequence to young ladies who are slighted by other men."

I heard every word, of course, during a break in the music, seated as I was not five feet away. It was all I could do not to burst out laughing. Such conceit! Such arrogance! When Mr Darcy was introduced to us earlier, I had been much taken with his handsome appearance, but it was now apparent that his manners and character did not reflect the near-perfection of his exterior. With relief, I saw him move off and allowed myself the softest of chuckles as I began to mentally compose a letter to my dear Papa, who would delight in the ridiculousness I had just witnessed.

When my aunt came to me shortly thereafter, I wasted no time in pulling her away to a private corner to relate the tale. Alas, it seemed Mr High and Mighty hails from the same corner of the kingdom as she, and she was too shocked that a Darcy of Pemberley could behave in such a manner to enjoy my story.

Jane's next set was free and, while Mr Bingley fetched her a cup of punch, I gave my sister to know what had occurred, hoping that she would laugh with me.

"Oh, Lizzy, I am certain he could not have meant it, or intend to be overheard," Jane said earnestly. "Such incivility could only be the result of some great strain or illness. Perhaps a sick headache."

Dear, dear Jane. Always so unwilling to believe that anyone could have aught but the best of intentions. I love her for it, but I sometimes also want to shake her for it, and this was one of those times. "If he felt too unwell to dance, why not simply say as much?" I enquired with a huff. "It was hardly necessary to do otherwise."

Jane sighed and gave me a stern, sad look which I knew to mean she thought I was being harsh for no reason. "People often behave uncharacteristically when ill," she said firmly, and I shook my head and knew that I would not convince her.

Mr Bingley returned, thoughtfully bearing a cup for me as well, which I sipped as they spoke. I was beginning to wonder about Mr Bingley, amiable as he was—tonight was the first time we had encountered any of his intimates, and I had found both his sister and his friend greatly lacking in courtesy.

I danced the fifth with a Mr Lowry, who was quite pleasant despite his conversation being confined to his love of springer spaniels and the kennels he maintained at his father's estate in Sussex. I like dogs and love to dance, so I enjoyed myself well enough. I caught sight of Mr Darcy once or twice, dancing at the head of the line with a blushing young lady who seemed better pleased with his company than he with hers. Bingley had engaged Jane for the supper set, while I had the pleasure of dancing with my uncle. We sat to the meal with my aunt and sister and the ever-present Mr Bingley, and made a merry party.

I did not think much of it when my partner failed to appear for the set which opened the dancing after supper; young men are not reliable creatures, and it was entirely possible he simply had not been able to locate me in the crush. My partner for the one following did not find me either, however, and I soon saw him moving down the dance with another young lady. I began to suspect that some mischief was afoot. To miss a set which had been promised was disappointing, but to seemingly be cast aside for a different partner was mortifying. Part of me wished to attempt to catch his eye as he moved down the dance, to perhaps discover from his response whether this had been a mistake or a choice. I certainly would have done just that in Meryton, but in this new society, among strangers, I did not feel I could. Instead, I pretended interest in a painting on the wall nearby, and attempted with moderate success not to squirm with embarrassment over having been so disregarded.

My aunt came to me as that set was ending. "Oh, my dear Lizzy," said she in a low voice, pulling me to the side for privacy—in truth, to the very spot from which Mr Darcy had pronounced me unworthy of his notice. "I am afraid you were not the only one to overhear Mr Darcy's comments. The Darcys are very influential..." She trailed off, appearing to search for words.

"And on the careless word of an important man, I am no longer seen as an adequate dance partner, is that it? You need mince no words, for I have already sat out two sets that were spoken for." I turned my dance card over, the names scrawled thereupon attesting to the accuracy of my recollection. My cheeks grew warm as I caught sight of the entries for the next sets and understood that it was unlikely those gentlemen would appear to claim me, either.

My dear aunt's face was a study in chagrin. "It would seem so. We may depart early, if that is your wish."

My chin came up; it is not in my nature to be cast down by the foolishness of others. "There are only two sets remaining. Let Jane enjoy herself, and let no one think I have been driven away by that haughty man."

"I have been standing too much this evening, Lizzy, but I see a pair of chairs just over there. Shall you keep me company?"

Her obfuscation was laughably poor, but I loved her all the more for the generous impulse which inspired it. "I can think of nothing I would like better. No doubt this will all be forgot in a day or two." I tried to believe that it would be so, and resolutely turned my attention to the pleasure of my dear aunt's company.

CHAPTER 4

FITZWILLIAM DARCY

Several days later, I was surprised by a call from Bingley just after my breakfast, at an hour at which I had rarely known him to be awake, much less active. Alarmed, I allowed my butler to show him into my study, where I had only just begun to attend to the day's business.

My friend entered with an air of great agitation, and having sat, he fidgeted for a moment before fixing me with a look of such pronounced disapproval that I believe I physically recoiled.

"Your comments about Miss Elizabeth Bennet at the Alvanley ball were overheard, Darcy," he informed me in clipped tones.

I searched my mind for a moment. I remembered the night of course but his words provided no illumination as to the circumstances. I had spoken of a young lady? And not in a manner of which my friend approved, by his demeanour. I hoped it had not been very bad; I was at times abominably ill-tempered at such gatherings. "I apologise, Bingley, but though the name is somehow familiar, I have no notion to what or whom you refer."

He gaped at me as though I had sprouted horns. "Miss Bennet's sister. Sir Edward's niece. The lady I suggested that you dance with early in the evening. You said she was not handsome, and that she had been 'slighted by other men'. She heard you, Darcy. She and others, at least one of whom was happy to spread it about. Though I only learnt of it the next day, none of the so-called gentlemen who had requested a set of her after supper came to claim their dances, and last night at the Winterbourne do, I was the only man other than her uncle who danced with her!

"By God, I wish I had never importuned you! But I am not the one who has turned society against Miss Eliz-abeth, and I would very much like to know what you intend to do about it."

Oh, Lord. He meant the dark-haired girl with the beautiful blonde sister who was his latest 'angel'. I recalled the lady now, and Bingley's little speech about my failure to dance. I passed a hand before my eyes, wincing as I understood that my uncharitable refusal had been overheard, and had caused her embarrassment beyond the moment itself. "I hope it will blow over in a few days," I told him hesitantly. "Something else will capture the attention of the quidnuncs soon enough, surely? I am sorry that she has been made uncomfortable by my unguarded speech, but I fear that any attempt to rectify on my part would only feed the gossip. Perhaps it would be best to let it lie until some more entertaining story arises."

"Well, I hope it may be so," he said with unusual sternness. "Miss Bennet is very upset over the treatment of her sister, and I do not like to see her upset. Miss Elizabeth presented a happy appearance last night, but I am certain that she suffered more than a little mortification."

If he was disturbed by the shunning of Miss Elizabeth, I was now alarmed by the apparent intensity of his attachment to Miss Bennet. He had been in love many times, and had even speculated on the possibility of matrimony once or twice, but he had never shown such protectiveness, and this for a lady he had known for perhaps a month. "You seem more attached than usual to your current flirt," I commented. This was, as it turned out, unwisely phrased.

"I will thank you not to refer to Miss Bennet in such a dismissive manner," he snapped, his expression darkening further. "I have never met a lady so suited to me, and when our acquaintance reaches a more appropriate length it is likely I shall offer for her."

"Pardon me, Bingley, I have only seen her once, and was not aware that you viewed her differently from the others," I replied in a placating tone which did not come easily to me. If Bingley's dubious expression was anything to judge by, I did not do it well, either.

"She is not like 'the others', as you call them, whose pretty faces and pretty manners were enough to captivate for a time, but not a lifetime," he replied after a moment, less heatedly. "She is genuine, kind, and intelligent. She even shares some of my interest in entomology," he related to my surprise. "She herself has made a study of botany, and her father keeps bees. She is familiar with all the species to be found on and around garden plants, and was interested to learn more of them from me."

He seemed quite proud of this, and though I risked raising his ire again, I felt I must express my own doubts, for his benefit. She would not be the first lady to have feigned a common interest to gain a man's favour. "Are you certain that her attention is for your insects, and not your income?"

His eyes narrowed sharply and that furious expression, so rarely seen before, returned. "Quite sure. She is not at all mercenary."

I attempted a placating tone again. "I do not know the lady as you do, and only ask out of concern for your happiness. You could do quite a bit better, you know."

"Could I?" he asked with a snort. "I might perhaps catch the daughter of an impoverished baron, or of a younger son, who would look down upon my lineage while happily spending the money my father drove himself into an early grave to earn. Miss Bennet is the daughter of a gentleman and the niece of a baronet, so no one could say I have not 'married up'. But her uncle, whom she loves, made his fortune in trade, and she is not in the least concerned that I have such ties. Sir Edward will give her two thousand upon her marriage, and she is to have another thousand upon the decease of her mother. Three thousand pounds is more than most ladies who would have me can boast. And more importantly than any of that, Darcy, is the simple fact that we suit." He sat back heavily after this impassioned argument, and there was little I could do but concede.

"Indeed, it seems your situations are not unsuited," I admitted. "And personal compatibility must outweigh a certain dearth of connexions. If you still feel this way for her when your acquaintance is of greater duration, I shall be pleased to dance at your wedding."

"Even with her 'tolerable' sister?"

"For you, Bingley, yes. Even that."

CHAPTER 5

ELIZABETH BENNET

Two nights after the humiliation of the Winterbourne ball, we attended a dinner party at which a marquess's younger son, who fancied himself an arbiter of society, declared that I hardly had a good feature in my face. I did not hear this directly, though I was aware from the moment of our arrival of the stares, whispers, and laughter my presence provoked. No, I learnt of this further indignity from Miss Bingley, whose glee was as ill-concealed as her sympathy was false. Why she should have any interest in me, for good or ill, I could not determine. I supposed she must see me as a rival for suitors, though she had a lavish dowry at which she hinted with tiresome and vulgar regularity. Then again, I possessed something which all her funds could never secure—a gentleman father. Perhaps that was the source of her dislike.

The next morning over breakfast, I suggested that perhaps I ought not attend the Frobisher ball that evening, concluding, "Mr Darcy's words might be sooner forgot if I am not before society as a reminder."

My aunt immediately objected. "My dear girl, I fear your absence would not have the effect you hope. You might rather be perceived as having been driven away. It could be tantamount to admitting that he was correct. I would urge you to reconsider."

The mere thought of another night spent pretending to be unaffected and unembarrassed wearied me. Pretending to enjoy oneself was, I now knew, very much more taxing than truly doing so. And yet, the notion of in any way confirming that conceited man's scornful words roused me to defiance.

Thus, to the ball I went, and having greeted my hosts, I retired to the chairs where the chaperons and wallflowers were already gathering. There I saw a well-dressed, prettyish young lady whom I had noticed at previous events but had never seen dancing. I selected a seat near hers, reasoning that neither of us would appear quite so isolated in such a configuration, and perhaps she might appreciate that small fiction as much as I.

During the second set, having surrendered Jane to another gentleman, Mr Bingley approached to secure my hand for the fourth. Having done so, he smiled and bowed to the other young lady. "Miss Downing, good evening. I hope you are well."

She replied that she was, and he asked whether she and I had been introduced. Upon learning that we had not, he happily performed the office, adding cheerfully, "You are both, to my certain knowledge, lovers of books, and therefore sure to be great friends." With this, he excused himself to speak with an acquaintance.

I indicated the empty chair next to Miss Downing and asked if I might keep her company for a time, unless she was expecting any particular friends to join her. She replied that I might, and we were soon speaking with each other quite easily. She pointed out her mother, ensconced in a large cluster of matrons, and her brother, Mr Vernon Downing, moving easily through the dance. Her father, I learnt, was surely in the card room. In my turn, I pointed out my own relations, and then we spoke of books as Mr Bingley had suggested. Jane and the Gardiners were all introduced to her over the course of the hours before supper, but aside from the set I danced with Mr Bingley we spent most of our time in each other's exclusive company.

When the supper set concluded and the crowd began exiting the ballroom, Mr Downing came to fetch his sister and looked surprised to find her laughing with me. He and I were introduced, and then we separated to attend our own family parties. As I entered the dining room, I witnessed my new friend up ahead, leaning heavily upon her brother for support, moving with a slow, lurching gait. I suddenly understood why I had never seen her dancing, and could only admire her cheerful demeanour at an event such as this.

Miss Downing and I found each other again after the meal, and I took it upon myself to draw two other young ladies into our orbit. Miss Walton was the granddaughter of a viscount, afflicted with spots, crippling shyness, and a very pretty younger sister also out; Miss Prentice was descended from the younger sons of several noble lines, but was an acknowledged bluestocking and, she admitted openly, rather poor. Miss Prentice entered into our banter readily, and after a time Miss Walton ventured to assay a comment or two.

Mr Downing approached us and was introduced to our new acquaintances, and gallantly secured the last three sets of the night, one with each of us. During our set, he thanked me for befriending his sister, commenting that he had never seen her enjoy herself so much at a ball. "But Mother will insist," he added wryly. "She drags Harriet to every event, convinced that one day some fellow will sit next to her and fall madly in love. And I hope it shall happen! Yet it seems to me that a ball is a most unlikely place for it."

"A mother's heart is forever hopeful," I replied, "or so I have been told many times by my own, who has never, I assure you, missed a single opportunity to put any of her five daughters into company. Whether that has been entirely to our advantage or not, I leave for the world to decide."

He chuckled and, in a tone of mock terror, said, "We must never allow your mother and mine to meet. They would be unstoppable together."

I left the ball feeling well-satisfied with my evening, having danced two sets and made four new acquaintances. Miss Downing had invited us all to call in two days at her father's house on Curzon Street, and I looked forward to seeing them again soon.

That visit was agreeable indeed, and I had the pleasure of returning with my family the following evening for a dinner party held by Sir Walter and Lady Downing, her parents. There I also spied Mr Darcy for the first time since The Incident, as I thought of it. Fortunately, he was seated at the opposite end of the table, and in the drawing room afterwards, Miss Downing and I retreated to a quiet corner to speak once Jane and I had entertained the company with a song. I was quite sure he had not noticed my presence, nor recognised me if he had.

CHAPTER 6

FITZWILLIAM DARCY

A fortnight after my blunder at the Alvanley ball, I was obliged to attend another, for it was being held by my aunt, Lady Matlock. Entering the familiar anteroom, I was surprised to see Sir Edward and Lady Gardiner and their nieces being greeted by my relations.

When I reached my uncle some minutes later I remarked that I had been unaware of the acquaintance. "Oh, yes, excellent fellow. Not at all what I expected." He lowered his voice to a more confidential volume. "We are near an agreement for an investment in his company. In a year or two, I hope to have the funds to reopen the east wing at Matlock!"

My own appointment with the shipbuilder had been put off the day before it was to occur, and I had heard nothing further. I determined to approach the man and enquire. In the ballroom, I saw few of my preferred acquaintance and chose to greet my eldest cousin,

Viscount Deane. We spoke of nothing in particular until something across the room caught his attention.

"I had heard that the wallflowers of London had banded together, but I had not expected them to be so jolly about it," he commented with a chuckle. I followed his gaze to a rather motley assortment of young ladies who laughed together with an ease which belied the fact that they were objects of general scorn. I recognised the spotty Miss Walton, the lame Miss Downing, the impoverished bluestocking Miss Prentice, the smallpox-scarred Lady Julia Moore, and...Miss Elizabeth Bennet? My stomach dropped into my shoes.

"It was the plain Bennet's doing, I heard," Deane continued. "Good for them, I say. Might as well get some enjoyment out of the occasion. And we won't have to feel guilty for not dancing with them if they are happy!" He guffawed at his own joke, and failed to notice that I was not laughing with him.

"The plain Bennet?" I repeated.

"Aye, there's the plain Bennet and the handsome Bennet." He gestured vaguely towards Bingley's lady, who was surrounded by eager young men. I knew that Bingley had not been invited, and thought vaguely that I ought to observe how she behaved in his absence.

"I do not think Miss Elizabeth Bennet plain," I ventured. I had observed her, really observed her, for the first time, at the Downings' dinner party, and found that she was not lacking in attractions. Her eyes were remarkably fine, her figure light and pleasing, her smile captivating. She played well and sang excellently, and though she had not the extraordinary beauty of her elder sister, she was no less than a beauty in her own right.

"That is what everyone calls her," Deane said with a shrug. "The way I heard it was that shortly after they came to town, someone highly placed declared her too plain to dance with, but said her sister was the handsomest lady in the room."

My stomach exited my shoes and made for the centre of the earth. My hopes that my incautious speech would swiftly pass from the attention of society had not been realised. Instead, matters were patently worse than they had been when Bingley chided me for it.

As it was my aunt's ball, I was required to dance more than I would have preferred. I partnered the daughters of my aunt's particular friends, and of my uncle's political cronies. Between, and often during, those sets, I observed the Bennets. Miss Bennet was gracious to all, but she did not seem delighted by the surfeit of male attention. I rather thought her somewhat ill at ease. Certainly the flirtations of her dance partners were returned with nothing beyond courtesy. She danced every dance, but often made her way to her sister's side between sets.

Miss Elizabeth appeared to be having a grand time with her odd assortment of friends. There was much laughter from their corner, and at times the ladies' heads were so close together they might have been touching. She danced the fourth with Mr Downing, who also obliged his sister's other friends, but no other gentleman approached her. She took the meal with her aunt and uncle.

These observations subjected me to an uncomfortable confusion of feelings. I knew from Bingley that Mr Bennet's estate was small and that this was the first opportunity his eldest daughters had been granted for society beyond that of the country and Sir Edward's mercantile set. It was surely their best chance to make good marriages, and in a moment of pique I had possibly blasted the prospects of the younger. That I had not meant to be overheard, nor expected that my casual judgment would prevent her acceptance by those among whom she now moved, had no bearing on the matter—it had happened, and I was to blame.

On the other hand, the lady did not seem at all downcast. Perhaps she did not care to marry yet, or was fond of someone near her home. If that were the case, all she had lost at my hand was the chance to make some well-placed acquaintances, and to appear often in the dance.

I approached Sir Edward late in the evening. Having exchanged the usual pleasantries, I was pleased by the man's civil demeanour. I had wondered if he would be angry with me, despite Miss Elizabeth Bennet's evident unconcern for the talk, but he was all politeness.

"I hope," I said, "we might reschedule the appointment which was postponed. I remain very interested in The Gardiner Company."

"Do you? I am surprised," he said, eyebrows raised.

"A man in your position must have many opportunities to choose from."

"I do, but some are clearly more promising than others. Will it be possible for us to meet?"

"You may expect a message from me tomorrow, Mr Darcy," he replied evenly. Pleased, I wished him a good evening and moved away, convinced by the civility of the uncle and the merriment of the niece that I had not really injured her at all.

My butler delivered the expected note from Sir Edward personally when it arrived the next morning. I hoped the business might be completed soon, for I very much wished to return to Pemberley.

> *Mr Darcy,*
>
> *Pray pardon me for not contacting you following the cancellation of our appointment. I had expected that you would understand why it was done, but it seems I must be candid. I will not be meeting with you. I am in no humour at present to offer opportunities to young men who slight my beloved niece.*
>
> *In all sincerity,*
> *Sir Edward Gardiner, Bt.*

I must have read it thrice before the message penetrated, at which time I recall laying it down upon the desk with great care, as though it might rear up and bite me if mishandled. I left my seat then, to look out over the street and the park as shame and indignation warred within me.

My pride revolted at having been so summarily

dismissed by a tradesman, his recent elevation notwithstanding. My conscience, contrariwise, insisted that his loyalty to his family was just and admirable–unlike my dismissal of his niece which had been quite the opposite. I was not in the habit of considering myself mistaken, but nothing could justify my words about the lady, even had they not had such an unexpected effect.

I began to pace the room. I had been so certain that the matter would be a minor *on dit* for a few days before passing from all memory. It seemed I had not correctly reckoned my own power at such a gathering, populated principally by those slightly beneath the Darcys and the Matlocks. I was so accustomed to paying no attention to those with whom I was not closely acquainted that I had forgot they might be paying particular attention to me. *That is a mistake I shall not make again*, I vowed to myself. *Henceforth, all my speech in public will be carefully considered. No man is perfect, but I shall learn from this, and be better than I have been.*

I had at least the satisfaction of knowing that none had been materially harmed by my error but myself.

Late in the daylight hours, I was surprised to receive my eldest cousin. Deane sauntered in and dropped casually into the chair across from me, smiling across the desk's gleaming top.

"Well, Darcy, you have put your foot in it this time," he commented without pausing for the usual civilities.

"You will want to avoid Pater for a time. He's excessively put out."

"I have not the pleasure of understanding you."

"Came to warn you. He has learnt it was you who insulted Sir Edward's niece—you might have mentioned that when we discussed the matter! Now he fears that his connexion to you will lead to problems with his investment."

I did not much care for the relish in my cousin's tone, but he only smiled more widely when I frowned.

"Pater has vowed to make it right, and I have been ordered to dance with the girl tomorrow at the Burnett-Bellingham ball—say that five times fast," he digressed with a chuckle. "Dead set on finalising this business, is the old man, and the house of Matlock will be lending its consequence to the plain Bennet until Sir Edward is happy, even if I must dance with her at every opportunity until Christmas."

I had considered the matter settled too soon, it appeared. "I had not the least notion of my comment being overheard, you know, much less spread about."

Deane looked at me as though I had lost my wits. "Have you been out in society all these years without realising that every word uttered by wealthy, unmarried men of a certain status is heard by somebody? There is no escaping the attention until you marry. But you may save your apologies until after I have endured half an hour with the girl. If she's insipid or worse, you shall have to do better!"

"Do you think... Ought I attend and dance with her myself? Would that appease my uncle?"

"I expect it would, yes. Shall we collect you on our way?"

Reluctantly, I accepted that I would be attending my second ball in the course of a week. "Pray do."

CHAPTER 7

ELIZABETH BENNET

Well before the dancing was to commence, I and my empty dance card were ensconced in a corner with Miss Walton, Miss Prentice, and the newest addition to our happy little band of revellers, Lady Julia Moore. Miss Downing had another engagement, but we made a pleasant foursome now that Miss Walton had become more comfortable, and voluble, with us.

I noticed Mr Darcy appear and groaned inwardly. Was I to meet him everywhere? Over a week had passed between our first, disastrous, encounter and his attendance at the Downing party, and I had hoped that we would move largely in different circles. This wish was beginning to appear ill-founded.

I turned my attention away from the insufferable man and back to the conversation of my friends, who were far more deserving of my consideration. I soon found my spirits rising once more and entered into our talk with real enthusiasm, until the approach of a pair of gentlemen silenced us all.

Mr Darcy bowed. "Lady Julia, Miss Walton, Miss Prentice, Miss Bennet, good evening. Are you all acquainted with my cousin, Viscount Deane?"

Lady Julia said that she was and poor Miss Walton, frightened into silence, nodded jerkily. Miss Prentice and I were not. Jane and Mr Bingley approached just then from another direction, and with the viscount's agreement were included in the introductions.

Lord Matlock's heir was a handsome, fashionable man of thirty or a little older, I judged, dressed well in colours more cheerful than his sombre cousin favoured. Between the two men there was no great resemblance save for their notable height, lean builds, and the pleasingly masculine shape of their mouths. The viscount was tawny-haired and blue-eyed, while Mr Darcy was as dark of hair and eye as of clothing. He also spoke with great ease and no little charm, while his cousin remained silent after making us all known to one another.

After some minutes of general conversation, Mr Darcy abruptly broke in to address me. "Miss Elizabeth," he said, fixing me with an intense, impenetrable look. "Would you do me the honour of dancing the third with me?"

Everyone else fell silent and all eyes turned to me. I smiled up at him, and saw him shift his weight in preparation, no doubt, to bow and depart until the appointed time.

In the brightest, most pleasant tone I believe I have ever contrived, I answered, "No, thank you."

CHAPTER 8

FITZWILLIAM DARCY

Now it was not only our party which had gone quiet. It felt to me as though silence rippled out from the centre of that group, that smiling young woman, freezing me to immobility as it passed.

My cousin's face split into a broad grin. "I hope, Miss Elizabeth," he said jovially, "that you will reconsider, for if you are not dancing this evening I should be very sorry to miss the chance of a set with you."

"As delightful as that would be, my lord, I am unable to reconsider my decision. Mr Darcy has done me a great favour, you see. He has allowed me to know which among my many new acquaintances are genuine, and which care only for appearances. The latter no longer associate with me. I could not possibly repay him by allowing him to subject himself to a dance with a lady he admittedly does not care to partner. It would embroil him in just the sort of falseness from which he has been so good as to shield me."

Deane leaned closer with a captivated expression. "Then you mark him as one of the genuine ones, do you, Miss Elizabeth?"

"Why, Mr Darcy is the most honest man in London, I am perfectly convinced. So much so that even civility has no claim upon him," she declared merrily, those beguiling eyes sparkling as she shredded my pride and my traitorous cousin roared with laughter.

"Madam, I am determined!" he declared. "I shall not attempt to persuade you further with regard to this evening, but when next we meet I shall claim that set." Her ready assent was another blow to my dignity.

"Come, Darcy," Deane said, and the promise of escape spurred my feet into movement, though I cannot recall if I even bowed to those we left behind. With every step I was conscious of the many eyes upon me, and the susurrating tide of whispers which followed in our wake.

CHAPTER 9

ELIZABETH BENNET

"Lizzy, that was unkind," Jane chided in her mild way once the two gentlemen had passed beyond hearing. "And now you shall not be able to dance at all."

I was not at all repentant, and refused to pretend to regrets. "I shall miss only my usual set with Mr Bingley, assuming he meant to ask. Mr Downing is not here, and no one else would have offered."

"Mr Darcy did, and Lord Deane would have."

"Mr Darcy wished to dance with my uncle's influence, and his lordship, I believe, was only trying to assist his cousin. You know that Uncle is displeased with the man, and so am I! I shall not help Mr Darcy recover my uncle's esteem. He may do that some other way, without reference to me. He has referred to me quite enough for one lifetime."

"Oh, brava, Miss Elizabeth!" laughed Lady Julia. "Surrender not an inch, for gentlemen are far too accustomed to having their own way."

"Darcy is not such a bad fellow as you seem to think," Mr Bingley interjected pleadingly. "I am sure he only said such outrageous things because he did not wish to dance. Perhaps he had the headache."

The perfect symmetry of the excuses he and Jane had invented made me want to laugh, but their insistence on taking that man's part killed the joke as soon as it was born. "He is not so bad to you, I am sure," I answered carefully. "But I have experienced his behaviour to those he deems beneath his notice and I cannot like it. If a gentleman does not wish to dance, or has the headache, he says so. He does not insult those who have done nothing to him. Your friend would do well to imitate your gentleman-like manner, Mr Bingley."

He did not look satisfied, but neither did he continue to defend his friend. The first set began to form, and he led Jane off to join it.

My aunt hurried up to me during the third, interrupting a lively discourse on novels. "Lizzy, everyone is saying that you refused to dance with Mr Darcy when he asked."

"It is true, Aunt, and I am unrepentant. As I told Jane, I believe he wished to return himself to my uncle's good graces, and I will not be used in such a manner."

"Perhaps he hoped to nullify the effects of his earlier remarks."

"I am sure he did, and equally certain that it was not for my sake but his own. He had no wish to make amends four nights ago at his own aunt's ball, but now that my uncle scorns him, his inclinations shift. No, Aunt, I believe I may safely assure you that I shall never dance with Mr Darcy."

"And I applaud you for it," interjected Lady Julia. "Perhaps this will be a salutary lesson for him."

"Be it as you wish, Lizzy," my aunt replied doubtfully. "If you are happy to bear the consequences of your refusal, I shall say no more."

CHAPTER 10

FITZWILLIAM DARCY

I had taken myself to the opposite corner from that in which the wallflowers congregated, and through the shifting mass of dancers I glowered at Miss Elizabeth Bennet. She had made a spectacle of me and there was little I disliked more. To the small voice which whispered that I had made a spectacle of her first, I was not yet prepared to listen.

There she sat, talking and laughing with her friends, free of cares, while I was forced to lurk even more on the fringes than I usually chose. Did she not appreciate the honour of my request, when I rarely danced and never with one of such low status? That the daughter of a country gentleman, unknown to society, the niece of an elevated tradesman, should refuse Fitzwilliam Darcy of Pemberley...

"Ah, a fine woman, that. If I were not so happily yoked, I might regret not having waited to meet her."

I startled as my cousin appeared beside me, his smiling gaze fixed upon the object of my angry thoughts. I felt myself frown. "She has made a laughingstock of me."

Deane grinned. "Disliking the flavour of your own medicine, Cousin? I have no sympathy for you. Few young ladies would have the courage to turn the tables on a man of your stamp, and I applaud her for it. I have just been speaking with Lady Gardiner—a charming woman —and discovered that I may claim my set with Miss Elizabeth at Lady Godfrey's do in only four days. I am all anticipation."

"I would call it spite, rather than courage," I grumbled.

"Perhaps spite gave her courage," he answered with a shrug. "I am not unfamiliar with the emotion myself, and she has every reason to spite you, you know she does. It does not lessen her achievement—she has taken the great Fitzwilliam Darcy down a peg. If my aunt and uncle were still with us, what would they think of your treatment of her? For my part, I believe they would applaud her as I do."

The image of how my gracious mother and impeccably courteous father would have reacted to learning of my public scorning of Miss Elizabeth deflated my fury. They would have been disappointed in me, saddened by my incivility and lack of consideration, would they not? Some of this uncertainty must have touched my expression, for Deane was now all sympathy.

"Next time you offend a lady," he suggested, "try apologising first."

"The request for a set was meant by way of an apology."

"Ladies need words, Darcy. They are not like us."

CHAPTER 11

ELIZABETH BENNET

Lady Godfrey's ball marked a slight change in my circumstances with regard to society. I had hardly set foot in the ballroom when Viscount Deane bowed before me, begging the pleasure of the supper set, to which I consented. Any number of people witnessed him putting his name to that important vacancy on my card and escorting me over to Miss Downing. I danced the second with Miss Downing's brother, the fourth with Mr Bingley, and as the viscount escorted me to the floor, I blushed under the many eyes upon us.

He soon put me at ease, for he was a fine dancer and an easy conversationalist. We spoke freely of town and country, fashion and literature, and of Lady Deane, who was in London with him but, being in expectation of an interesting event soon, could not go about. He impressed me with his evident affection for his lady, and I realised with a start that he was the first man I had found in

London–excluding my uncle, of course–who seemed to enjoy the married state.

He escorted me into supper, where we sat with Lord and Lady Matlock, his parents. The lady was a bit chilly in her manner, but his lordship was pleasant and welcoming. We continued our conversation over the meal, including the earl and his countess, and my genuine interest in the prodigious talents of the viscount's two-year-old son seemed to effect something of a thaw in Lady Matlock's demeanour.

Returning to the ballroom, I was introduced to Sir John Hatton, a baronet of about five and thirty who requested a set of me. He was handsome, well-dressed, and charming, and his presence across from me in the dance earned me more than one look of envy. He enquired about my father's estate and spoke a little of his own, between and somewhat south of Bristol and Bath. Of the latter city we also spoke, for I was curious and he had visited many times, though he called the society there 'stifling'.

At a dinner party a few days later, I encountered him once more, and was pleased to receive his attentions in the drawing room, after the meal, where we spoke of literature and theatre. At another ball, he danced with me twice and partnered me for supper, and after a fortnight during which we met often, I began to feel that my heart was in some danger despite the gulf in our ages and stations. He seemed equally smitten, so I did not worry over the rapidity of the attachment, instead drinking in his stories of his estate and his young son and daughter, privately wondering how they might react to a stepmother.

I continued to spend a great deal of time with my new friends. Miss Downing and Lady Julia, wallflowers due to physical defects rather than any lack in their families, taught me a great deal about how society truly worked, as opposed to how it presented itself. I longed to introduce Miss Prentice to my father, for her sardonic wit and wide knowledge of literature were very like his. Miss Walton was a dear soul who put me in mind of what Jane might have been, had she not possessed great beauty to lend her confidence.

Jane's romance was coming along excellently well. She and Mr Bingley were a golden couple, attracting admiration and envy wherever they went. All wished to know them, it seemed, except perhaps his unmarried sister. She patently wished that he might court a lady of more prominence, but her brother was unmoved. He doted upon Jane, and when he learnt that there was an estate to let near Longbourn, spoke of taking it.

There was only one blight upon my happiness during this time, and it caught me entirely unawares. We attended a dinner held by Admiral Walton, an aged seaman long retired, who delighted in speaking with my uncle of all things nautical and naval. The subject of the current war and the ships which fought it featured heavily in their odd friendship, and so my aunt and Jane and I found ourselves surrounded by elderly men and their elderly wives, with only a few closer to our own age scattered among the company. One of those, unfortunately, was Mr Darcy, whose late father had some connexion to the Admiral.

I do not know why he came. He spoke to no one but his host, and to him very little. We were, fortunately, seated far enough apart that we could not be expected to converse, but amusingly, close enough together that I could overhear Lady Manningly sing the praises of her eldest granddaughter to him throughout the meal, a performance which only deepened his quotidian frown. Though I thought it a pity that such an insufferable man should be so handsome, it seemed fitting that he should display his ill-humour constantly, providing a warning to those who might otherwise think well of him for no reason but his descent and fine features.

In the drawing room Jane and I were pressed to perform, being the only ladies younger than my aunt in attendance. We obliged, and the ladies were kind enough to praise our efforts and insist upon encores until the gentlemen joined us and had an opportunity to hear a song also. When we were released from the instrument, I made it my business to keep at least half the room between myself and Mr Darcy. So intent was I on avoiding him that I, as our host would say, left my star-board quarter open for a volley.

I was cornered into an extended conversation with the ancient Earl of Telford, a hunched figure who insisted upon clasping my hand between his own damp palms as he greeted me, and professed to have greatly admired my performance at the pianoforte, and my contribution to the singing. He was curious about my life in the country, and questioned me minutely about my habit of walking Longbourn's lands. I bore his inquisition patiently, believing him a harmless old man, and thinking his company as good a shield against Mr Darcy as anyone's.

At last, he seemed satisfied with my answers, beaming at me in such a way as to display his few remaining tobacco-stained teeth, which themselves did not appear to be long for this world. "Ah, ah, excellent," he said in a hushed tone. "You are lively and active. Your stamina is no doubt prodigious. You play and sing beautifully." His eyes dropped to my bosom and lingered there as he continued, "I have a little house in Brompton, and within it a beautiful instrument which will delight you. There is a park across the road, where you may maintain your...vigour."

I felt the heat of his breath upon my chest as he relished the word, and took a half-step backwards. "I have no notion of what you speak, my lord," I said, though I rather feared that I did.

At last, he returned his gaze to my face, and in his rheumy eyes I saw a flavour of avarice that chilled me to my marrow. "Why, my dear girl, I will set you up there. You are perfect, exactly what I require. And having served me, you will find yourself much in demand when I am done with you. I am known for finding the best and finest new high fliers, and training them well. If you mind your pennies, you will be rich before you lose your bloom."

I believe only the shock of the application prevented me causing a scene by flinging my drink at his face.

Shock—and the knowledge that Mr Darcy would have yet more reason to look down upon me. I kept a hold of my cup instead, softly pronounced but one word— "Never"—and then pasted a smile on my face, stepped back, claimed in cheerful tones meant for other ears that I had taken too much of his time, and with an exactingly proper curtsey rid myself of his company and made for my aunt's side, where I spent the rest of the evening pretending to enjoy myself.

That was made easy by the fact that my proper place as a young lady in aged company was to show interest, nod, and smile. This freed me to consider what had so unexpectedly passed in a respectable man's drawing room, mere feet from his respectable guests.

I wish I could believe that such a disgusting suggestion was borne of senility, I thought, *but now that I have been deemed unworthy of the 'marriage mart', is it possible I am considered fresh goods in a less salubrious market, by so-called gentlemen who are not unduly burdened with a moral conscience, and who do find me 'handsome enough to tempt' them?*

CHAPTER 12

FITZWILLIAM DARCY

I avoided all social engagements for a fortnight after the debacle at the Burnett-Bellingham ball, spending more time than I wished pondering Deane's suggestion that my departed parents would be disappointed with how I have conducted myself, and coming to the lowering conclusion that it was certainly so.

That I had not intended to wound was immaterial; I had behaved badly, and contrary to the assumptions I drew from her happy manner, it appeared I had injured Miss Elizabeth Bennet. Upon reflection, I found much to admire in her response to her near-banishment from society. Rather than retreat to her country home or into silent humiliation, she had taken the opportunity to forge alliances with the other scorned ladies who lurked at the edges of ballrooms and parlours, and thereby to enjoy herself. It was clear that her new friendships were genuine, for the delight those ladies took in each other's company was too vivid to be feigned. She had made the best of an uncomfortable situation, something I had rarely attempted and never carried off.

Certainly I had not tried to make the best of the evening we met. I despised dancing and the avarice with which I was so often regarded by my dance partners and their relations. Add to that the ever-present thoughts of my sister's near-entrapment by a scoundrel, and I was in no humour to even attempt to enjoy myself. I understood that it was the duty of a gentleman in a ballroom to dance, but at some point, I knew not when, I had selfishly decided that such rules of proper behaviour did not apply to me. I found that I ignored the mores of society as it suited me, while remaining convinced that I was one of the better examples of gentlemanly comportment. My morals were certainly sound, more so than many of my acquaintance, but my manner was lacking, and I had not the least idea how to improve, for easiness in company had ever eluded me.

But, easy or not, plan in mind or not, I must do better. There was no other option, if I were to call myself a gentleman. And furthermore, I must make amends to Miss Elizabeth if such were possible. I must, at the very least, apologise. In words, as my cousin had so pointedly advised.

When I saw her at Admiral Walton's dinner, I hoped my chance had come, and during the meal I divided my thoughts between being properly attentive to my dinner partners and composing an apology. We re-joined the ladies after our port in time to hear another charming performance by the Bennets, but I was not able to secure her company for even a moment afterwards. She was damnably elusive, always in smiling conversation with someone or other. That old lecher, Lord Telford, kept her to himself for more than half an hour, and I was becoming concerned for her sensibilities when they parted at last, with smiles on her side and a curious expression of consternation on his. I was relieved to know that he had said nothing to overset her, but still I could not find a way to capture a moment of her attention for the communication I was so anxious to deliver.

Nearly a week passed before we were in company again, this time at a ball where she had all her friends about her. Neither my courage nor my pride would allow me to approach her before the company which had borne witness to our previous interaction, so I bided my time and waited for an opportunity. While I waited and avoided Miss Bingley, I saw Miss Elizabeth take to the floor several times: once each with Deane, Mr Downing, and Bingley, and twice with Sir John Hatton. Deane and Sir John had been good friends for a time, years before, but there had been a falling out and the two rarely spoke. He and Miss Elizabeth had seemed to enjoy each other's company very well, even engaging in some light, acceptable flirtation. A moderately wealthy baronet such as he would be a stupendous match for Miss Elizabeth, but the knowledge that Deane maintained only the barest acquaintance with the man made me uneasy.

I managed to separate my cousin from the crowd and asked, "Will you tell me why you no longer associate with Sir John Hatton?"

With a grimace of distaste, he replied, "Years ago, long before I met my wife, I was rather enamoured of a Miss Cole, who became Lady Hatton. After her marriage, we remained friends of a sort—as much as we properly could—until her death. She was very unhappy in her union, for Sir John was neither faithful nor discreet."

While infidelity was more the rule than the exception among men of the higher circles, it was bad form to shame one's wife, the mother of one's children, in that way. I understood perfectly why my cousin had distanced himself from the man; I had done the same, for the same reason, with several acquaintances of my own.

Miss Elizabeth Bennet did not strike me as the sort of lady to quietly accept such treatment, and I thought that in addition to my apology I might be able to do her a good turn through a quiet warning of her suitor's proclivities. I thanked my cousin for the information and returned to the ballroom to continue seeking an opportunity to speak with her.

My chance finally came when she left her friends to acquire a cup of punch during a set, while Sir John danced with another. I intercepted her at the otherwise deserted refreshment table, and there I asked her forgiveness for my weeks-old slight, and for not having made my apology sooner. To this, she replied with courteous acceptance, though I could see that my presence was unwelcome. There was more I felt I had to say before I released her, and so I hurriedly, quietly, spoke.

"Miss Elizabeth, I feel I must tell you something, so that you may...make any future decisions with all the necessary information. Sir John was not an ideal husband to Lady Hatton. She was made very unhappy by his...other interests. Some ladies are content with such an arrangement, but I would wish that you know what awaits you, should he make you an offer."

I could not determine whether her expression of disgust was for me or for my words, until she spoke. "And I am now expected to trust you, I suppose, over one who has never been anything less than a gentleman to me? I think not," she replied rather sharply, though quietly.

I stepped back and bowed, saying only, "Excuse my interference. It was kindly meant." I had done what I could. I hoped very much that she would not marry him. I should hate to see her bright spirit crushed.

CHAPTER 13

ELIZABETH BENNET

How dare he? I fumed inwardly as I returned to my friends. As though he were any judge of gentlemanly behaviour! I could not imagine Sir John behaving as alleged, and if by some chance it were true, he had been younger then, and he had hinted that his marriage had been one of suitability rather than sentiment. If he had sought tenderness elsewhere, I could not approve, but perhaps I could understand. He would certainly not behave so were he to marry for affection.

"I saw you speaking to Mr Darcy," Miss Downing murmured in my ear, as the others eagerly debated the merits of the early chapters of a novel we had all agreed to read together. "And you do not seem happy. Was he unkind again?"

I squeezed her hand. She was such a dear, and remarkably lacking in that bitterness most ladies would feel in her place. "No," I replied, equally quietly. "But he was rather infuriating, which perhaps he cannot help. He apologised for insulting me when we met—and I appreciate that—but then he had the gall to...to suggest that Sir John and I are not suited. Even had things progressed to such a point, he has no right to concern himself."

"I think there are few of whom Mr Darcy approves," she murmured. I nodded my agreement and, seeing that Lady Julia was regarding us with curiosity, turned my attention to the general conversation.

Sir John appeared as the penultimate set was forming and asked if I should care to take a turn about the room. I accepted with alacrity, for we had danced twice already, and as much as I enjoyed that activity, I preferred our conversations. For a full half hour, we strolled along the edges of the ballroom, speaking of Shakespeare and of Parliament, of our acquaintances who had gone to fight Napoleon and of autumn in London. All the while, I ignored the dark glower of Mr Darcy from his lonely place between a pillar and a plant.

Perhaps it was that which prompted me to raise a subject I never had before, when our time was drawing to a close. "I am surprised, sir," I opened lightly, "that you are willing to be seen so often in the company of a lady found unworthy by a man of high mark."

He laughed, a low rumble that made my stomach quiver pleasantly. His hand brushed the small of my back, but when it did not linger there, I concluded it had been an accident. "For all that we know many of the same people, Darcy and I move in different circles. He prefers the stodgy and staid, afternoons at White's discussing the price of wheat and evenings having as little fun as possible." His teeth flashed briefly, and I bit my lip against a laugh. "I prefer music, and laughter, and interesting people speaking of interesting things: literary salons where they discuss Sterne and Cleland, not Richardson and Johnson. I prefer people like you, who are not always pretending to either a fashionable ennui or a saint-like probity, and who have thoughts beyond the latest fashion or scandal."

I blushed and smiled at his praise, and agreed that my tastes were very like his, though I was a little uncomfortable that I did not recognise the authors he praised. I concluded that they must be current, even *avant-garde*, and put it from my mind. He returned me to my friends then, after relating with a wry expression that he was engaged for the last with the daughter of a friend of his mother's. I ventured a little quip about family obligations and was rewarded with another of his shiver-inducing laughs before he departed.

We met again only days later at a tea hosted by Lady Ganlon, and there he introduced me to his good friend Lord David Montmorency, the third son of the Duke of Leeds. His lordship seemed to approve of me, which I thought very promising. Though I could not say that I loved Sir John, I felt that it would be very easy to do so. Though our acquaintance spanned only a month, I considered that I might soon be in receipt of his proposals and was minded to accept. Never before had I met a gentleman whose conversation so beguiled me, nor whose mere presence caused a response deep within my body. Jane, in our whispered conferences in the darkness of our shared chamber, had admitted that merely being near Mr Bingley created a warmth and a sort of longing in her belly which had quite alarmed her at first. This, I took to indicate that the sensation was a sign of love, for if Jane was not in love, I had never witnessed the state.

I cherished a hope that Sir John would request the first at Lady Oglethorpe's ball the following evening, but he did not appear until halfway through the second. He was flatteringly quick to secure the third, however, and Lord David requested the fifth, as I had already granted the fourth to Lord Deane. After my recent experiences in ballrooms, three sets in a row quite went to my head, and I felt myself positively bubbling with good cheer. All of my partners were fine dancers and entertaining company, and by the end of the fifth I was puffing with exertion and laughter. Lord David kindly led me to the refreshments, where he procured a cup of punch, and then to a quiet place along the wall where I might catch my breath.

"I am usually hardier than this, my lord," I assured him, "but our assembly hall at home is rather more draughty than this lovely house, and does not become so warm!"

He grinned. "I have never considered a draught as an advantage, but now that you explain, I can only agree that it must be so, in that circumstance." He leaned forward confidentially. "Tell me, Miss Bennet—have you and Sir John come to an agreement? My friend is being remarkably close-lipped on the matter."

"We have not," I replied, and his broad smile confused me.

"Capital. I am glad I asked. I feared I had missed my chance. You see, Miss Bennet, though I have not my friend's independence, I do have more ready cash. I can keep you better than he, for I have neither children nor estate to support, and I maintain a fine set of rooms in Soho where you would be most comfortable. You would have no reason to complain of my generosity." His countenance expressed real security in my positive reply.

Before my encounter with Lord Telford, I might have been baffled by this offer. In that moment, I was almost grateful to the old man, for that distressing encounter allowed me to react swiftly to the surprise of this one. I drew myself up, placed my empty cup of punch into his hands, and as he tried to puzzle out why I had done so, I whispered, "I will thank you never to speak to me again. You, sir, are no gentleman."

I walked away from him then, struggling not to allow my fury to speed my steps and draw notice. I was not thinking clearly, which must be why I walked out onto the terrace alone, as I would have done at the assembly rooms in Meryton, though my aunt had several times reminded me that it was not advisable in London. It was deserted, however, for the night was chill and the wind biting. I relished the slap of cold on my heated cheeks, and drew in great lungfuls of frigid air to cool my temper.

"Miss Bennet, are you well?" Sir John came up beside me, brow furrowed with concern.

"No, sir, I am not. Your friend, Lord David, has just..." I drew a breath, and confessed the humiliating truth. "He has made me a dishonourable offer."

I was relieved to see the expression of anger which overspread his features. "I shall thrash him!"

"I wish you might," I agreed heatedly. "As though I should ever accept such a degrading situation."

He took my hand in his and spoke in gentle tones. "I sometimes forget how provincial your upbringing has been. You cannot have been at all prepared for London Society. But of course you shall accept an unconventional relationship—what else is there for you? It would be a waste of your wit and beauty to dwindle into a country spinster, or to be always a dependent in some relation's home. Even your incomparable sister has done no better than a tradesman's son. But I knew from our earliest acquaintance that you would be a bright light among the 'fashionable impure', and I mean to be the one who opens the world to you."

I stared at him in horror, my mouth agape, my mind entirely blank as all my dreams fell to ashes at my feet. "No," I managed to gasp, stepping back and trying to pull my hand from his grasp.

"Come now, sweetheart," Sir John cajoled, tightening his clasp and drawing me back towards him, then gripping my upper arms to keep me there. "Let me give you a taste of the delights which shall be yours." He bent his head toward mine, intent upon a kiss and I hardly knew what else, as I shook my head frantically, repeating my denial over and over.

"Hatton!" An angry voice broke into our struggle. "Unhand the lady."

CHAPTER 14

FITZWILLIAM DARCY

I had been with Deane, half-listening to his litany of evidence that his heir's intelligence was far greater than is usually met with, when I saw Miss Elizabeth Bennet remove herself to the terrace. She seemed upset, though I could not have articulated why I thought so. Moments later, I saw Sir John Hatton follow her, and my concern increased. If it were a planned assignation, would she not have seemed happier? I excused myself to Deane—I think I excused myself, at any rate—and followed as nonchalantly as I could. It would not do for me to blunder into causing more difficulties for her by being indiscreet in assuring myself of her welfare. The door was very slightly open, just enough to admit a bit of cooling air and to allow a person to slip through if they wished. I looked out, and what I saw fired my blood with rage.

Sir John held Miss Elizabeth by the arms, attempting to press a kiss upon her while she struggled, protesting, "No, no, no, no, no!" I was moving towards them before I knew it, and called upon him to cease. In his surprise, he did. Miss Elizabeth tore herself from his grasp and, with one wild look at me, ran back inside.

"Damn it all, Darcy, that was none of your concern," he berated me.

"It is the concern of every gentleman when a lady is importuned—I might even say, assaulted." I may have been shouting; I shook with fury. "You should thank me. Had you succeeded in forcing an embrace, it would not have advanced your suit."

"My suit?" Suddenly, the man was laughing. "If you thought I meant to wed her, you are as foolish as she. I would not take a leg shackle for a pound less than fifteen thousand. One does not marry pretty articles from the backwaters, Darcy."

I was shocked into silence by this speech. Low connexions and a smallish dowry she might have, but the girl was respectable. She was a gentleman's daughter and the niece of a baronet, and there had been nothing in her demeanour or behaviour to suggest any inclination towards immorality. But this man seemed to think that any girl outside the 'ten thousand' was fair game for debauchery.

A hand fell onto my shoulder. Deane's face was set into grim lines, and unlike me he had not lost the facility of speech. "I saw you come out here, and Miss Elizabeth Bennet exit shortly thereafter. I came to find out if you had offended her again, but I see something worse has occurred." He glared at the baronet, who smiled insouciantly.

He held up his hands, shrugging his shoulders. "I shan't trouble her again. She is outraged by my offer, the silly cow, and I am in no charitable frame of mind towards her—I have wasted weeks cultivating her acquaintance and affection, all for naught. I expect that if I were to try to make it up to her, the two of you would interfere. You may congratulate yourselves on saving her from a life of luxury and intellectual stimulation—I am sure she will thank you both when she is an ageing spinster in someone else's home."

My fist wiped the smirk off of his loathsome face before my cousin's could.

We left him there, cursing and mopping up his own blood with a handkerchief, and returned to the warmth of the ballroom. A few people saw us come in, but there is nothing unusual in a pair of gentlemen taking the air, and perhaps a cigar, in the middle of a ball, and no one seemed at all curious.

"I've a partner for the set about to form," my cousin murmured to me. "You will have to tell me all later." I nodded and he went in search of the lady, while my eyes sought Miss Elizabeth Bennet.

I found her near the refreshment table, clutching a cup of punch and largely concealed behind a particularly ugly piece of statuary. I made my way towards her casually, nodding to my acquaintances and presenting what I hoped was an air of idle boredom. I fetched up next to her at last and, looking out over the dancers, murmured, "Miss Bennet, are you well?"

She nodded once, jerkily. I ascertained that we were

unobserved before I quickly related, "Be assured that I will not speak of what has occurred. But please, if he should approach you again, inform me or Deane." I glanced at her, only to find her intently studying the contents of her cup. "I sense you would prefer a moment alone. Good evening, Miss Bennet." With that, I moved away, though I would continue to observe her discreetly for the rest of the evening. She spent a while longer in hiding, then emerged to join her friends in their corner. She appeared entirely at ease, though I knew she could not be so, and I greatly admired her fortitude.

CHAPTER 15

ELIZABETH BENNET

I had not dissembled when I told my relations, on the road to London, that I truly did not expect to marry. I had little dowry, no great connexions, and middling accomplishments. If my sister's extraordinary beauty had not yet garnered her a serious suitor, then what chance had my own more common charms to evince such an improbable result as the affection and hand of an estimable man?

And yet, though I hardly acknowledged it even to myself, the dream persisted. Hope is a base and feral creature, slinking through the darkness to devour any scrap that may sustain it. It will survive the most dreadful calamities, and its claws deal sharper wounds than reality ever could.

Even when I was relegated to the fringes of society it had not seemed quite impossible that some good man might see past the disdain of one insufferable fellow and his many eager hangers-on and say to himself, "There is a woman I could love. There is the lady with whom I would most wish to spend my life." But I now felt that it was impossible, that it had always been nearly so, and that slim chance had been quite banished.

I hated Mr Darcy and Sir John Hatton with every fibre of my being. I hated the former for pulling that cracked door so firmly shut, and the latter for tearing that vicious, mauling hope away and leaving me bleeding inside. And I hated more than anything that I must feel grateful to the insufferable Mr Darcy for coming to my aid. It was particularly galling to recollect that he had not only warned me about Sir John, but had been witness to the results of my refusal to heed that warning. My humiliation was complete indeed.

I do not recall how I got through the remainder of that interminable evening. I must have put on quite a convincing display, else my aunt and sister would have been swiftly at my side enquiring after the cause of my distress. But once within the sheltering darkness of the carriage, I could feign contentment no longer.

"I wish to return to Longbourn," I said. "Tomorrow, if at all possible."

My relations could not be content with merely knowing my wish, of course. They must understand why I wished it. Eventually, when we were safely returned to my uncle's home and the servants had been excused from the parlour and the door closed, I reluctantly told them, learning several interesting phrases from my uncle in the moments following these revelations. Jane was too occupied with weeping to take in his profanities, but my aunt hushed him and, once convinced that he had himself under good regulation, undertook to see my sister to our chamber, leaving us alone.

My uncle poured himself a generous measure of brandy and, to my surprise, set a modest dram before me. A sip of the fiery spirit paradoxically helped to somewhat cool the rage that burned hot inside me. I now understood why gentlemen were so quick to reach for the stuff when unsettled.

"Your aunt and sister were too shocked by Sir John's offences to notice, I think, but I clearly heard you refer to 'such insulting offers', Lizzy," he said gravely. "I will have the name of any other man who has importuned you in even the slightest way, and I will have it now."

I felt my cheeks heat. I had hoped to keep the humiliating secret that the man I had thought to be courting me had not been the only one to think to use me so, but my uncle was too quick and canny. As briefly as possible, I described the other two incidents, and watched as he grimly drained his glass and filled it once again before he was able to meet my eyes.

"I wish, more than anything, that there was something I could do to address these insults," he said angrily. "But against such men, I am powerless. None of them have sought to invest with me, and anything else I might seek to do would likely get me hanged."

"I do not wish that you should harm yourself or your business on my account," I replied with alarm, "though I appreciate your desire to avenge my honour. I want only to return home and try to forget that any of this occurred."

He rubbed a hand across his face and regarded me with regret. "I cannot send you home, not yet. Your father wrote to instruct me—after I informed him of your difficulties in society—that no matter how bad it got I was to keep you here until after the first of December. You see, Longbourn has a visitor—Mr Collins, your father's cousin and heir. It seems he came with the idea of mending the breach in the family by marrying one of the daughters of the house he will inherit, and he was not pleased to find only your younger sisters in residence. Kitty and Lydia are too young and silly to marry, and he has been disappointed by Mary's lack of beauty. If you were to return to Longbourn, your father fears that he would instantly fix upon you, and distressing scenes would arise when you refused to marry such a pompous, stupid man as he describes."

I listened to all of this with astonishment, and it was some moments before I felt sufficiently in command of myself to reply sensibly. "I do not wish to go about in society any longer, Uncle. If I may not return home, tell me that I may stay quietly here."

He was quick to agree and soon, my head swimming with all that had occurred, and perhaps a bit with brandy, I retired for the night and was, for once, happy to see that Jane had preceded me into slumber.

I woke, late and alone, to a grey day with fat snowflakes meandering lazily downwards amid the rain-drops. It fit my mood perfectly. The rage of the night before had cooled to a hard lump of grief in the centre of my chest, and it felt as though all the long years of my future stretched out before me, as cold and bleak as the view from my window. I lay abed pondering my few options for a considerable time before there was a soft knock upon the door, and my aunt peeked inside.

"Ah, you are awake," she said with a gentle smile, and entered carrying a tray with a pot of tea, a little dish of eggs, and one of the orange scones she knew I favoured. This she set upon the bedside table, saying, "I thought you might like the treat of breakfast in bed."

"I am not hungry," I replied, though I sat up and accepted the cup she prepared for me.

"Have a bite of the scone, at least."

Unwillingly, I obliged her, and my capitulation seemed to loosen her tongue. She fixed me with a kindly look and said, "Lizzy, my dear, you have had a great disappointment, far worse than the usual sort which befalls a young lady. I expect that you are feeling very silly for being so deceived in him, but you must recall that we all liked that man, we all believed he was on the verge of an honourable offer. Your uncle and I are astounded that he would court you so openly, to such a purpose."

I looked down at my hands, surprised to find that half the scone was gone. I placed the rest upon the tray. "If I had accepted his offer," I reasoned as I spoke, "and gone off with him, my family would have to put it about that I was ill, and in time that I had died, to save my sisters' reputations. There would be little that Father or Uncle could do against him. If anyone asked Sir John about me, he would need only say that our flirtation had ended.

Those who share his proclivities would know the truth, but they maintain their own reputations by concealing such activities. There was no reason not to lure me with what seemed a respectable courtship. It was the only thing which could have drawn me in."

My aunt shook her head wearily. "Such wickedness. One does not like to think it possible, but I can readily bring to mind the names of a dozen young ladies who appeared in my own circles over the years, only to vanish due to illness or the needs of an elderly aunt in some far-flung place. In some cases, I am sure that was the truth, and of course, some simply found themselves with child through their own foolishness, but now I must wonder how many were enticed into such a life as you were offered."

"Aunt, I am so ashamed," I confessed miserably, "for I can understand why a girl might accept such an offer. He raised not only my affections, but...other sensations."

"Oh my dear girl." She clasped my hands. "It is natural, entirely natural, to feel an attraction of the body. Wrong to act upon it outside of marriage, of course, but such feelings are ever so much more common than love. It is romantic to think that only the man we love could stir such feelings within us, but that is hardly ever the case."

Her words were a comfort to me, though it would be many months before I could recall without a shiver of disgust how I had once longed for the moments when his hand would brush mine, or his shoulder touch my own as he murmured in my ear.

"Has my uncle told you why he will not return me to Longbourn?"

"Yes, and I have seen your father's letter on the subject. Mr Collins sounds like a great buffoon, slavishly devoted to his patroness and neglectful of his duties to the rest of his flock. Your mother is desperately attempting to convince him to wed Mary, but he is reluctant, having seen your youngest sisters' beauty and hearing of yours and Jane's."

"I wonder..." I bit my lip, then nerved myself to continue. "Perhaps I should go home. If he likes me, Longbourn would remain in the family, and Mama and my sisters would be assured of a home." Love and happiness I felt beyond my reach, but the satisfaction of a duty done was not, and I was not unwilling to grasp at it.

"No, Lizzy," my aunt snapped, as vehemently as I had ever heard her speak. "You shall not throw yourself away for Longbourn. I had rather anything than see you make yourself unhappy to do what your father, by rights, ought to have done—see to the futures of his wife and daughters."

"I understand that the marriage itself might not be congenial, but would I not find fulfilment in aiding my family, and happiness in my children?"

"The happiness of motherhood and that of a good marriage are very different, yet they are intertwined!" she declared. "You need look only to your own mother to see how difficult it may be to find joy in children when there is none in the marriage. But Lizzy, I feel that you are giving up on the idea of love simply because your first attempt has ended badly. It is not like you."

"I have never thought it very likely that I should find the love I wished for," I admitted. "Look at Jane. For all her goodness and beauty, she has not had a true suitor until now. What hope have I?"

"Every hope in the world," my aunt insisted. "You are every bit as lovable and deserving as your sister, though I concede that it may be a little more difficult to find a man who will appreciate your intelligence rather than be threatened by it. I felt very much as you did before I met your uncle, you know, and I had a disappointment or two of my own before that fortunate day. Do not allow that man to harm you more than he already has. He deserves no such prominence in your thoughts or your actions."

I was very much struck by the notion that I was allowing Sir John to determine my future, and though I could not share her optimism, I promised that I would think seriously upon her words.

CHAPTER 16

FITZWILLIAM DARCY

I did not see my cousin again for a week, not until I visited to congratulate him on the arrival of Lady Helen Fitzwilliam, the first daughter born into the family since my own sister. Though bursting with pride in his little family and relief that Lady Deane had come through the ordeal swimmingly, he did not forget to quiz me on the subject of Miss Elizabeth Bennet. I explained to him what had transpired before his arrival on the terrace that night, and he had a few choice words to say on the subject of Sir John Hatton. He commented that he had seen Sir Edward, his wife, and his eldest niece on two occasions before his wife was brought to bed, but that Miss Elizabeth had been present for neither.

Immediately upon leaving my cousin's home I called upon Bingley, where I found no relief for this new concern. Once we were able to extricate ourselves from Miss Bingley's attentions on a pretence of business matters, I asked after the Gardiners and Bennets and learnt that though all were in health, Miss Elizabeth had declined to appear in society any longer.

"Miss Bennet has been quite uncommunicative about the matter," he mused, seeming no less worried than I. "Sir John is no longer in the picture, that is all I know. I have seen Miss Elizabeth when I called, and she seems in very low spirits."

"I am sorry for it, and sorrier still for my own part in her troubles. I hope, rather than believe, that they are not connected."

Bingley looked at me in some surprise, then frowned. "You think that he may have thrown her over due to her lack of popularity?"

"Something like that, yes."

"Ridiculous! She is as fine a lady as I have ever known!" he protested. "Sensible, good-humoured, and devilish clever, not to mention nearly as pretty as her sister." He drummed his fingers on the desk for a moment, and then added, "I hope very much that she will soon be my sister."

"You have made your decision, then?"

"I have. Do you think that you and Miss Elizabeth will be able to get along?"

"Certainly, for my part. Whether she will be able to abide me, I cannot say," I replied. I squelched the impulse to again attempt to talk him out of marrying a lady of little distinction; speaking against a Bennet had already gone spectacularly wrong, and I was in no mood to chance a repeat. Let Bingley make his own choices, and live with them. It seemed unlikely that he would be unhappy with such a gentle creature, after all.

I saw the Gardiners and Miss Bennet at a card party held by a distant relation of mine two days later. Though I only bowed to Sir Edward and his wife from a distance, I boldly approached Miss Bennet, despite Bingley's absence, and rather awkwardly mentioned that I had hoped to see Miss Elizabeth with her.

Miss Bennet smiled as though I had said something entirely wonderful. "I will be sure to tell her that you asked after her, Mr Darcy. She has decided that she does not much care for the social whirl," she added delicately, "but her friends are always welcome to call at my uncle's home. Miss Downing and Lady Julia visited us earlier today."

I wondered if Miss Bennet had forgot that her sister certainly did not consider me a friend, but suspected that she had simply chosen to believe my enquiry meant that all was forgiven between us. I was not so sanguine, but the idea of calling upon Miss Elizabeth, of seeing for myself how she fared and perhaps attempting to further mend matters, took root in my mind. I deliberated over the notion for several days more before resolving to risk the very real possibility of being turned away.

When I presented my card at the large, handsome house on Gracechurch Street, the door was not shut in my face. I was instead brought upstairs to a finely appointed room where Lady Gardiner greeted me with perfect civility. We spoke for some minutes—it transpired that she had spent much of her childhood not five miles from my own home—before I felt myself able to enquire after Miss Elizabeth.

"She is in good health," the lady replied.

"So I have been told; but with you, I will be open and confess that I have been concerned for her state of mind since her confrontation with a certain gentleman who does not deserve the appellation. Indeed, I feared that he might have bruised her, for he seemed to be gripping her arms very tightly."

I soon understood that I had blundered again. Lady Gardiner knew nothing of a confrontation, or of my presence during it. She knew only that the man had made her niece a dishonourable proposition, and had been refused. I had little choice but to inform her of what I had witnessed. That she was displeased was evident, but her wrath was reserved for the scoundrel, and she thanked me most graciously for my intervention and subsequent silence, and requested that I pass her gratitude along to my cousin, also.

I soon took my leave, for the atmosphere had become stilted and it was clear that Lady Gardiner was distracted by what I had disclosed. I regretted that, as I regretted not coming to know the ladies of this household sooner. They were, each of them, estimable beyond the common way, and I felt that I had by my early behaviour relinquished the opportunity of a closer acquaintance than being tolerated as Bingley's good friend.

As I approached the bottom of the stairs, a door opened to what a quick glimpse suggested was a comfortable family sitting room, and the object of my visit emerged. "Miss Elizabeth," I said, hurrying the last few steps to bow before her. "How are you?"

Surprised, she made a perfunctory curtsey. "Mr Darcy. I am well, thank you."

But I could see that she was not well. She was pale and drawn, with dark hollows beneath her eyes, which displayed none of the sparkle I had so admired. I was entirely determined not to fail in civility, and said, "I am glad to hear it, and more happy still to have the privilege of your company. Unless I am keeping you from something?" Belatedly, I had heard from the room behind her the murmur of voices.

She glanced almost guiltily towards the door, standing open a hand's-breadth, then fixed me with a look I could only call challenging. "Mr Bingley hinted that he should like a moment alone with my sister. I obliged."

"Ah." I fought the urge to fidget with my cuffs or cravat. "If...if things are as you suspect, I believe your sister will be very happy. My friend is an excellent man, and will no doubt be the best of husbands."

Her expression softened. "And Jane will no doubt be the best of wives. I believe your friend, too, will be very happy."

"I am certain of it. Your sister is everything good." This earned me the first genuine smile I had ever got from her, and brief as it was, it warmed me. "Will your family be happy for them also, or will they be disappointed that Bingley has no estate?"

"My father will be sorry to see Jane leave Longbourn, but he will be pleased for her. My mother will be ecstatic

—with five daughters, no son, and an entailed estate, it has been the purpose of her life to see us all married. Though realistically, she will probably have to settle for Jane and perhaps one of my other sisters. We have little to recommend us."

The resignation in her voice disturbed me, for it sounded nothing like the lady who had so cheerfully braved the scorn of society. Guilt smote me. My sins against her were nothing to Sir John's, and yet they had opened the way for his disgusting behaviour. "Surely you cannot think that you will end a spinster? With your wit and vivacity, a gentleman father and a baronet for an uncle, and what I understand to be a respectable dowry, it is inconceivable."

She shook her head. "I have received all the offers I am likely to, sir, and my greatest hope now is that I will be invited to live with my dearest sister."

The certainty in her voice struck me a blow that sent me reeling, and as though from a great distance I heard myself say, "I could marry you."

She stared at me for a long moment, and I am sure I stared back with equal, if not greater, shock. Then she huffed out the ghost of a laugh. "I am tempted to accept," she commented in a peculiarly detached tone, "and plague you all your days. But I shall not. I have always been a happy sort of person, and I hope to be so again. Marrying for spite would not restore me to myself."

"I would make it my business to assure your happiness." Even as I said it, I wondered why I was pressing the point. I knew only that I felt I must.

The look she turned upon me then was frankly incredulous. "My happiness would be your business? How cold you are." Her arms crossed over her chest, as though holding her own warmth close. "I thank you for the honour of your proposal, sir, but I must respectfully decline." She turned and slipped back into the sitting room, and I had no words to arrest her departure.

CHAPTER 17

ELIZABETH BENNET

I returned to find my sister and Mr Bingley holding hands and staring at each other in the most besotted manner. They were quick to inform me that they were engaged, though they wished it to remain between us until they had secured my uncle's blessing. Jane was two and twenty and required no one's permission, not that I believed for a moment that either my uncle or my father would have refused it in the face of her transparent happiness.

It was not until late that night, alone in my bed with Jane dreaming blissfully in hers mere feet away, that I had a chance to think over that encounter at the foot of the stairs. Mr Darcy had proposed marriage! Or near enough, I thought wryly. It had been more a statement of fact: he, an unmarried gentleman, could marry me, an unmarried woman who was no relation of his, if we were both inclined. I did not really think he was any more enamoured of the notion than I had been. Rather, I felt he was trying to atone for the insult which had, as it were, separated me from the flock and left me vulnerable to such wolves of society as I had then encountered. A lifetime was a heavy price to pay for a moment of incivility, however, and I did not think that being married to a man who did not really want me would be a congenial fate, either.

Once my anger had cooled, I had begun to see Mr Darcy differently from before that fateful evening. For all his arrogant conceit, I had come to accept that he was likely a good man, perhaps even a very good man. I did not for a moment allow that he, who had surely been pursued by fortune hunters for years, would have entered a darkened balcony which he believed to be deserted. It would have created too delicious an opportunity for just the sort of trap he surely wished to avoid. Therefore he must have gone out there for a purpose, and as Sir John and I were the only people there, it was logical to conclude that he knew or suspected as much and had followed us. Given his earlier warning about the man, he may even have done so out of concern for me.

When confronted with such a scene as had been enacted there, most people would have simply retreated back inside rather than become involved, and most of those would have immediately begun to gossip about it. Not Mr Darcy. He had involved himself, to my benefit, and I had seen him return to the ballroom with his cousin —how he had come to be there was a mystery to me— some minutes later. What had transpired in those minutes I could not know, but I expect he and Sir John argued, as men will do when their tempers are roused.

As for gossip, there had been none. My relations assured me of this every time they returned from an outing—not a word was being said of me or Sir John, except that he had abruptly closed his house in town and there was some speculation that our 'romance' had ended in a quarrel. Mr Darcy, it seemed, had said nothing, and whatever the viscount knew, he had been likewise silent.

That is, Mr Darcy had said nothing until today. My aunt had got me alone for ten minutes and delivered a thorough scolding on concealing from her and my uncle that the knave had dared to lay hands upon me. To be fair to Mr Darcy—and I was trying to do so, though I had not yet released all of my resentment—he likely assumed that they already knew. My aunt certainly believed that I should have informed them, and perhaps she was correct. I had been wrong about so much of late, why not this?

The next day after dinner, my uncle summoned me to his study, where he sat contemplating a letter. He regarded me gravely over the top of it before folding it up and setting it on the desk between us. "I was astonished to receive today a letter within a letter, from Mr Darcy." He studied my reaction to this cryptic comment for a moment before continuing. "The first page was addressed to me, and in it he requested that I give you this, after reading it myself if I wished." He tapped the pages he had set between us with a fingertip.

"Mr Darcy has written me a letter?" I said rather stupidly.

"He has. And I have read it, and will allow you to have it, but only because I recently learnt of his actions in removing you from a desperate situation—which you ought to have told me of yourself."

I opened my mouth to defend my secrecy, but what could I say? I said nothing.

He stood, nudging the letter towards me. "I suspect you remained silent from humiliation as much as any other motive. But in the future, you must inform the man in whose charge your protection rests of any such events." He gazed sternly down upon me until I nodded my acquiescence. "I shall leave you to read your letter, then."

Alone, I hesitated to take up the missive. What could Mr Darcy have to communicate to me that was so important as to involve my uncle, with whom he had no good relationship? The only way to find out was to read, and so at last I opened it.

Miss Elizabeth Bennet,

I do not know why I always seem to say precisely the wrong thing to or about you. I have begun to suspect it is not a problem unique to you, and that you have merely been the unfortunate person to finally bring a lifetime of gaffes to my attention. But whatever the case may be, if I cannot trust my tongue to convey my meaning, I will give my pen a chance.

Please, allow me to apologise for my outrageous suggestion yesterday. I was so eager to make amends that I did not consider to what sort of amends you would be receptive. What is the point of trying to atone for one's mistakes if one does not take the wishes of those one has wronged into the highest consideration?

I ought to have said: I am so desperately sorry for what I said of you the night we met. It was done in a moment of childish petulance of which I am deeply ashamed. I had not even looked at you closely enough to form an opinion of your attractions, and since that night I have come to consider you one of the handsomest women of my acquaintance, and one of the most admirable. I have never been able to laugh at the vagaries of society, or at offences against myself, as I have so often seen you do. Your spirit humbles me.

I wish I had followed my friend's advice and asked you to dance that night. How much sooner I would have known you for the estimable lady you are. We might even have become friends, and I sincerely mourn the loss of that opportunity, almost as much as I mourn the price you have paid for my insolence.

There is yet more I should have said yesterday. I ought to have told you of my sister. She will be sixteen in February, and despite her youth I think you and she would be great friends. You are both able musicians and lovers of books. Her temperament is not unlike Miss Bennet's—self-effacing and kind. And she was only months ago, at her tender age, importuned by the slyest sort of fortune hunter, who injured her confidence and her vulnerable heart in cold-blooded pursuit of her dowry. You and she both know what it is to be deceived for a man's selfish purposes.

Despite everything I have done amiss, regardless

of all my missteps, I will dare now to ask: Will you agree to be introduced to my sister's acquaintance? I am certain it may be managed in such a way as to require you to tolerate my presence only rarely. I pray you will consider the notion, and will demand no more of your attention, though I remain,

Your servant,
Fitzwilliam Darcy

CHAPTER 18

FITZWILLIAM DARCY

The shock of being refused had carried me home and into my study with hardly a thought in my head. There, free of the need to pretend that all was well, I became angry. To be so quickly dismissed by one whose condition in life was decidedly beneath my own was appalling. I had offered her more than she could ever rightly expect in marriage—status, connexions, wealth, a fine estate. What further sources of happiness could she require?

Although...

I had possessed those very things all my life, and I was not happy, was I?

She had been raised on an obscure estate, in a family of no note and little wealth, but she was by her own account and my observation 'a happy sort of person'. Or she had been, until the chain of events I set in motion had brought her low.

'How cold you are.'

Her words chased themselves around my head, and I

began to see how I must appear to her. Always so careful to show no weakness to those eager to exploit such to their own advantage, to someone like her—open and genuine—I must appear devoid of every proper feeling. Certainly my behaviour on our first meeting gave her ample reason to dislike and distrust me, but even had I not spoken so, what in my demeanour or manners would have given her cause to view me in a positive light? I wondered, suddenly, how many other good people, how many more potential friends, I had driven away by trying and convicting them of unworthiness, without evidence.

Several days passed after I had left my letters with Sir Edward, and I began to conclude that either he had declined to give Miss Elizabeth hers, or she had declined to reply. A more definitive answer did at last come from Lady Gardiner, and its contents astonished me.

Mr Darcy,

My nieces and I would be delighted to receive you, and to make the acquaintance of Miss Darcy.

Here, she listed several days in the next fortnight when they expected to be at home, and offered to reserve any of them for our visit, if I would only let them know which, at my earliest convenience.

We look forward to meeting your sister and to knowing you better. We hope that before long we will all be good friends, as we have become with your own friend, Mr Bingley.

Yours sincerely,
Lady Gardiner

I saw what I hoped was Miss Elizabeth's hand in those words. I was to attend, not only my sister, and it was hoped that we would all be friends. Surely Lady Gardiner would not express such wishes without Miss Elizabeth's approval. I was to have one more chance to demonstrate to her that I was not always an unmitigated churl.

I wasted no time acquainting Georgiana with the fact that I wished to introduce her to Sir Edward's family. She was not as reluctant as she usually is, for she had heard of them from Bingley and owned to a curiosity about the Miss Bennets and their relations. Having secured her agreement, it was then necessary that I swallow my pride and inform her that she must not expect to find anyone there who thought particularly well of her brother. I explained what I had done and how it had affected Miss Elizabeth's time in society, ending with a reference to a gentleman deliberately engaging her affections while not believing her worthy of his hand in marriage.

"Poor Miss Elizabeth!" she gasped after some moments of shocked silence. "Brother, how could you?"

"I cannot justify my actions, and will not attempt to. But I will tell you, as I told her, that I believe you and she have many inducements to genuine friendship, not the least of which is that you have both been injured by the schemes of dishonest men."

"You cannot have told her of Ramsgate!"

"I said only that a fortune hunter deceived you in hopes of securing your dowry. If you should ever wish that she know more, that must come from you. Nor have I told you all I know of her disappointment, for it is her story to share or withhold as she sees fit."

"And you would allow me to tell her more, if I wished?" she asked uncertainly. My cousin Colonel Fitzwilliam, her other guardian, and I had impressed upon her that the incident at Ramsgate must be kept concealed from society, so her reticence was understandable.

"I believe that she, and also her sister, could be trusted with the information," I answered carefully. "Unlike many, they do not delight in spreading the misfortunes of others."

With Georgiana's agreement, a message was dispatched to Lady Gardiner accepting the first of the dates she had offered, and on the appointed day we presented ourselves in her parlour, where I introduced my sister into her acquaintance and that of her nieces. The Miss Bennets quickly drew my sister aside and set about making her comfortable, while I spoke with Lady Gardiner.

"Thank you for allowing this," I told her. "My sister is in great need of sensible, good-hearted friends."

"Is not everyone?" the lady replied with a smile. "In this, I will admit, I was guided by my younger niece," she added, giving weight to my hope that I had not lost all hope of gaining some measure of Miss Elizabeth's esteem.

"She is generous," I murmured, smiling as I watched

my sister hide a giggle behind her hand. I returned my attention to my hostess, picking up the thread of our previous conversation on the subject of the village of Lambton and its manifold charms. A little later, Miss Bennet called her aunt over, and Miss Elizabeth vacated her chair for Lady Gardiner's use, taking up a place near me.

"And how are you today, Mr Darcy?" she asked graciously.

I swiftly decided openness and humility would be my best course. "Much better, for having been readmitted to your presence," I replied, "though I do not know that I deserve the honour."

Her eyes widened, but she replied with apparent composure, "I am grateful to you, sir. Your intervention was most timely. And if you continue to bring your charming sister around, I might well forget that I ever disliked you," she concluded with a twinkle in those remarkable eyes.

I glanced at the others, finding the younger ladies engrossed by whatever Lady Gardiner was saying. "I confess, I did not quite know what to make of your aunt's invitation. It seemed to suggest that I was welcome, but my sister could easily visit with her companion in future, if you prefer, and I could make myself scarce if you wish to call upon her."

"I see no need for that. If you are willing, we might begin again."

CHAPTER 19

ELIZABETH BENNET

When Mr Darcy agreed that we might begin again, I had no notion he meant to take it so seriously. I hoped we would be civil, even friendly, for his sister's sake and that of Jane and Mr Bingley. He, however, seemed quite determined that we become true friends. Our return to Longbourn was postponed indefinitely, for my sister chose to marry from my uncle's house rather than subject Mr Bingley to an uncomfortable stay at the Lion Inn in Meryton. My mother wrote Jane a long, unhappy letter complaining that she was not to enjoy Christmas with her most beautiful daughter, nor to be allowed to plan her wedding. When Jane wavered Mr Bingley had only to whisper in her ear and she found the strength to hold firm.

Miss Darcy rarely called without her brother, and when we called upon her in Grosvenor Square, he was sure to be there. He always found a few minutes to speak with me, and my early impression of him as a dark

Adonis come down from Olympus to sneer at us mere mortals was quickly replaced by that of a quiet young man, perhaps too inclined to gravity, who often had to be cajoled into joining the conversation, but always listened to what was passing with focused and flattering attention.

At my uncle's home, he often seemed more at ease than at his own; I attributed that to Miss Bingley. Jane liked Miss Darcy as well as I did, and we called upon her together. Whither went Jane, there also went Mr Bingley, and when our destination was Darcy House, Miss Bingley followed her brother and made herself ridiculous in her constant attempts to draw her host's attention. That he was made deeply uncomfortable by her efforts was plain to everyone but her.

One afternoon a fortnight before Christmas, Miss Bingley was particularly insistent upon his company, hardly allowing anyone else even to speak with him, drawing him aside and nattering away until the poor man looked entirely miserable.

"Charles," I said in a low voice—it was strange to address a gentleman so informally, but it made him so happy to feel as if he were my brother already that I could not do otherwise—"I think Mr Darcy is in need of a respite."

He glanced at his friend and grimaced. "I keep trying to slip out of the house without her, but she seems able to read my mind when it comes to him. Poor Darcy, he has had worse than Caroline scheming for his notice since we were at Cambridge, and likely before. I would not have his position for all the wealth in the world."

Here was a thought: Mr Darcy must feel himself as much the prey of the more unscrupulous members of society as I had, and likely more so. It could not be a source of wonder if he had not wished to be introduced to yet another young lady who might be one of them. Though his insult of me had been most uncivil, it had not been personal, and the consequences had been far beyond the scope of his intent. All of this flashed through my mind in an instant, and though I would consider it in depth later, I set it aside for the moment.

"May I send her to you?" I asked my future brother, and he reluctantly nodded. I stood and approached the pair, and though Miss Bingley did her best to pretend that I was not there, she did eventually have to draw breath, and Mr Darcy was quick to ask if I required anything.

"I do not, I thank you, but Mr Bingley wishes a word with his sister," I replied, smiling, and had to stifle a laugh when Mr Darcy's shoulders slumped in relief as she ungraciously released his arm and moved away. "I am very glad," I said to him in low tones, "that Jane is not the only one with ridiculous relations, else I should be afraid ours would frighten your friend away."

He looked surprised. "I cannot imagine to whom you might refer."

"Oh, I thought he might have related to you what my sister has told him of our family. Even Jane knew a word of warning would be necessary." I smiled wryly. "You will meet them at the wedding, so you might as well know that my two youngest sisters are wild and undisciplined, the other prosy and severe, my mother loud and vulgar, and my father too amused by their antics to exert his authority. Several gentlemen have expressed an interest in Jane over the years, but they have all been quickly driven away by Mama's encouragement."

"I...I confess I cannot imagine you or Miss Bennet having such relations. You are both so perfectly genteel." He fixed me with an earnest gaze, and I felt my pulse thrum in my breast—much as it had done that day when he had stepped towards me in my uncle's vestibule and insisted that, if I were to marry him, he would work for my happiness. I had put it down to anger then, but I knew better now. Mr Darcy was a very handsome man, and a very good one, and I was not immune to his appeal.

I scrambled to marshal my scattered thoughts. "You may thank my aunt for that. When my youngest sister was born, my parents were told there would be no more children, and therefore no long-awaited heir. My mother's nerves overcame her, and Jane and I, who were old enough to understand some of what was passing, were sent to live with the Gardiners, who had been married only a few months. We would spend much of the next several years with them, until Mama felt she could have us all at home once more. In that time we were greatly influenced and, as you have seen, we maintain a close relationship with them to this day."

"You could have had no better example than Lady Gardiner," he replied in his grave way. If I had not come to know him better these last weeks I might have thought it mere courtesy, but now I could recognise the sincerity underlying his solemn tone.

"No, we could not," I agreed. "We have some slight hope that being among unfamiliar company will check my mother's and sisters' exuberance at the wedding, but you should probably expect to be horrified." I covered my own unease by making the suggestion in an impudent manner. Though he smiled as I had intended, I suspected that he had seen through my pretence.

"I have an aunt," he offered, "who is loud and domineering, and unwilling to hear any opinion other than her own. She has spoken for years of her wish that I marry her daughter as though it were a settled arrangement; with that and other questionable opinions, she contrives to mortify me whenever we are in company together. Every family, I think, must boast some ridiculousness, if only to guard against hubris."

I laughed at that, he laughed with me, and even Miss Bingley's poisonous glare could not check us.

CHAPTER 20

FITZWILLIAM DARCY

I could only conclude that I was the most idiotic of fools. I had openly insulted a lady, destroyed her acceptance in and enjoyment of society, made her a clumsy and ill-advised proposal of marriage which she had rightly refused, and then I had gone and lost my heart to her.

The question was, what did I mean to do? I saw two choices before me. I could disengage from our acquaintance, as much as possible with my friend betrothed to her sister, and attempt to conquer my sentiments. This is what most of my family and friends would expect, if they knew of my struggle. Though she would not be a terrible match—daughter of a gentleman, niece of a baronet, modest but respectable dowry—neither was she, in those terms, at all what I was expected to secure. Yet Elizabeth was so much more than antecedents and fortune, and it was her other qualities, her courage and good humour and capacity for forgiveness, and yes, that beauty which I had early denied, which had turned my head, seized my heart, and led me to seriously consider the second option: attempting to win her hand.

Could I possibly succeed? It seemed unlikely. Though she had brought herself to accept my acquaintance and, I dared to believe, my friendship, could her pardon possibly extend to trusting me with her future? There was, of course, only one way to know for certain. One fraught and terrifying way.

I was wrong. I did not have two choices. I had only one. I could not give her up without making the attempt.

It was my aunt, Lady Matlock, who gave me the chance to begin, amusingly enough. She was a little too impressed with her own consequence, the daughter of a knight who had risen to the title of countess, and she disapproved of my uncle's warm friendship with the Gardiners. She would be aghast to know that I had a personal interest in one of their nieces. But when she conceived of the idea of holding another ball, she again allowed her husband to persuade her to invite Sir Edward and his family, and I then suggested including the Bingleys for Miss Bennet's sake. With Deane's encouragement, she eventually agreed.

When I called at Gracechurch Street with my sister several days later, I had with me my aunt's invitations, which I was pleased to deliver. "My aunt is having a ball on Twelfth Night—rather intimate, as much of her preferred acquaintance are too far from town to attend—and you are all invited," I explained, handing the cards to Lady Gardiner and Bingley.

Later in the visit I seized the opportunity of a private

conversation with Miss Elizabeth while my sister sat at the instrument with Miss Bennet turning the pages. "I wondered if you would be so kind as to dance the first with me at my aunt's ball? If you do not wish to, we shall forget I asked, and you will not be obliged to sit out," I hastened to add.

She regarded me for a moment before smiling and saying that she would be delighted. The relief I felt was indescribable, and spurred me to say, "And if I may be so bold, might I request the supper set also?"

Now she beheld me with unrestrained wonder. "The first and the supper set? People will think you wish to court me, sir."

I could meet her bright eyes no longer, so I dropped my gaze to my hands, which were twisting together in a nervous and most inelegant manner, and said, "They would not be wrong."

CHAPTER 21

ELIZABETH BENNET

I did what I always do when I feel uncertain: I made a joke. "Am I now to believe that I am more than merely tolerable?"

He laughed, to my great surprise, shaking his head and saying, "Pray, do not remind me of what I said then. I would dance every set with you, were it possible." He smoothed the front of his waistcoat, inadvertently drawing my attention to the fact that no evidence of indulgence marred the lines of his form or the finely tailored clothes encasing it. "Miss Elizabeth, I have done everything backwards with you. A gentleman is supposed to charm a lady on first acquaintance, and only after securing her affections should he vex and torment her."

I nearly choked on my own laughter at that unexpected jest, delivered with such grave sincerity that I had not anticipated it. He seemed rather pleased with himself, and it became him very well.

"You may have the supper set," I conceded when I

could speak again. "But I do not know that I wish for more than dances."

He regarded me curiously, but said only, "Is that not the purpose of calling—to convince you, if I am able, that you wish for even more of my company? I am not easily deterred."

I hoped rather than believed him to be so steadfast. The notion that Mr Darcy, of all people, admired me was astonishing, and it strained credulity to think that an association which had begun so poorly might end in a happy marriage. It must also be acknowledged that I was reluctant to risk my bruised heart again. If he harboured any such doubts, he concealed them well. From that day he began to openly pay me the most flattering attentions his native reticence would allow. My aunt was puzzled, our sisters delighted, Mr Bingley astonished, and my uncle uncomfortable with this development, but they all did us the courtesy of allowing us to determine our own fates, and aside from ensuring the strictest of chaperonage, left us to come to know one another better.

My relations and I passed a noisy, happy Christmas Day—courtesy of my young cousins—and a quiet Boxing Day. The twenty-seventh brought us to Darcy House, where Mr Darcy attempted to engage me in conversation with Miss Bingley clinging determinedly to his arm. Had she been even slightly pleasant, I should have felt sorry for her, but she was not, and I did not. My aunt and I shook our heads over her clumsy advances on our way home, and even Jane had nothing to offer in her defence.

CHAPTER 22

FITZWILLIAM DARCY

I had always thought the business of courting would be an easy thing—select the lady, pay her attention, make my proposal, wed. That, I saw clearly once I had embarked upon my quest to win the hand of Miss Elizabeth Bennet, had been sheer conceit. Certainly it could have proceeded in that manner had I chosen one of the ladies who were always speaking and acting for my approbation, but I had selected a woman worthy of being pleased, and I would be required to do so.

She challenged my ideas at every turn. It was at times, I think, for the sheer pleasure of debate, but we had diverging views on many things. Had we not been inclined to please, we might have quarrelled viciously more than once, but as it was, we listened to each other and more often than not we both moderated our views and came, if not to agreement, then to a more harmonious understanding. I thought it boded well for a future together, feeling that by her good humour and compassion, my tendencies towards distrust and cynicism might be softened, and through my greater knowledge and experience of the world, her idealism might be tempered. A union between us would be of great benefit to us both. I had only to convince her of it.

There was also the problem of being allowed to get on with my wooing in peace. This was not difficult at Sir Edward's home, for though he still regarded me with suspicion, he did no more than warn me that he would not tolerate seeing his niece wounded again, and watch me closely when we were in company together. The problems arose at Darcy House, for as delightful as it was to see Elizabeth in the home of which I hoped she would soon be mistress, I could hardly ask that she visit with only her aunt and leave her elder sister at home. Unfortunately, when they visited, Bingley always appeared to see Miss Bennet, and Miss Bingley always appeared to see me. Though she had never discerned my disinclination for her company, she was quick to spot my inclination for Elizabeth's, and she became more forward and difficult with every day that passed.

Desperate as I was to simply enjoy having Elizabeth in my home, I was equally determined never to fail in civility before her again. I endured Miss Bingley's antics as stoically as I could, used those visits to forward my sister's friendship with the lady I hoped would become her sister, and dared to dream of a day when no one could come between me and the woman I loved ever again.

CHAPTER 23

ELIZABETH BENNET

Lady Matlock's ball was on Twelfth Night, but it was not a masquerade ball. In London, Mr Darcy informed me, masked events had a tendency towards debauchery, of which his aunt and uncle did not approve. This was a relief to Jane and me, partly because we had not wished to spend more of my uncle's money on costumes when he had been so generous with our wardrobes already. On the appointed night, we got ourselves up in our very finest, and my aunt loaned us some of her more modest jewels.

Matlock Place was alive with candlelight and swags and wreaths of greenery, the air scented with the fruits and spices of steaming bowls of wassail, mulled wine, and hot punch. The earl greeted my uncle and aunt as old friends and bowed avuncularly over my hand and Jane's, saying that we would have all the young bucks agog. Lady Matlock greeted us with more restraint, as was her way, and wished us a pleasant evening.

All of my small circle of friends had left London for

the winter, so I remained by my aunt's side for a time after Mr Bingley whisked Jane away in pursuit of a cup of punch and, no doubt, some semi-private conversation.

My aunt was soon pulled into a group of matrons, and I found myself in the too-familiar position of standing at the side of the room, observing. The musicians were quietly tuning their instruments, and the dancing would soon begin. I had not yet spied Mr Darcy, though I felt an inexplicable confidence that he would appear for our set.

"Miss Eliza, I am surprised to see you here." Miss Bingley had appeared at my side. I thought to myself that she would be quite pretty if she did not insist on always frowning haughtily or, as at that moment, smirking in a superior manner.

"I do not know why you should be. My uncle has become a good friend of his lordship's."

"Yes, he has certainly taken advantage of this opportunity to raise himself above the stench of trade," she said condescendingly.

"And few would understand that as well as you," I replied with a like tone. "What was it your father manufactured? Cloth?" If Miss Bingley wished to play the 'superior status' game, I was more than willing to oblige her.

Her jaw tightened and her colour rose. "But to return to my original comment," she said repressively, "I was not surprised to see your relations, only you. You have hardly been seen for over a month, and to take pleasure in a ball, partners are required."

"I thank you for your concern, Miss Bingley, but I

take as much pleasure in conversation partners as in dance partners. And as it happens, I shall not be without the latter. I have three sets reserved, one of them with your brother."

"Oh, well, I am glad you will not sit out all night, to be sure."

"And you? Have you a partner for the first, perhaps?"

"No, but I am to dance the second with Sir Walter Elliot."

"Well, there is a little time, you may yet be asked."

"I plan to spend the set in conversation with Mr Darcy," she declared. "It is a long-standing arrangement between us, you see. He never dances the first. All of London will know he is as good as engaged if they ever see him take to the floor to open a ball." She gave me a look of exaggerated sympathy. "I am sorry if this disappoints you, but so it is."

"Not at all," I replied complacently, though inside I was already laughing at the shock which was barrelling down upon her.

"Ah, and here he comes. I expect you will wish to join your aunt now. I do thank you for keeping me company."

Mr Darcy stopped before us and bowed, offering his greetings. Then he turned to me, offering his hand. "Miss Elizabeth, I believe the line is forming. I hope you had not forgotten?"

I smiled and took his hand, waving the other between us, setting my dance card to swaying on its ribbon about my wrist. "Not at all. You may inspect my card—I wrote you in as soon as I received it."

He smiled broadly, drawing the startled glances of several persons nearby. "Shall we, then?" He nodded to my slack-jawed companion. "Miss Bingley."

We took our places in the line, to the apparent amazement of many, and the music began. We danced well together, though without conversation at first. I made a comment that others would think it strange if we passed the whole dance in silence. He smiled and said, "I have been wondering what it was that made you wish to laugh as we joined the line. You had some difficulty in suppressing it, I think."

Did he know me so well as to perceive as much, when usually only my father could see that which I cared to hide? It seemed he did. But his mention of it made me want to laugh once more, and I shook my head, promising I would enlighten him during the break. We had then a little conversation, but I found that simply dancing with Mr Darcy was interesting enough, and I did not much care what anyone else thought of our periods of silence.

The first dance of the set ended, and as he escorted me to the table for a cup of punch, I discreetly gave him to know that just before he had joined us, Miss Bingley had declared that he never danced the first. I did not repeat what else she had said, for it would have seemed as though I were inviting a declaration.

What I did reveal, he found amusing, and then he

leaned down and said, almost in my ear, "I have never before wished to dance the first."

I am quite sure I was still rather flushed when, some minutes later, we took our places for the second dance of the set.

CHAPTER 24

FITZWILLIAM DARCY

I had always believed myself entirely disinclined towards dancing, but now I knew that I enjoyed it very much indeed with the right partner. Having Elizabeth's flashing eyes and light figure across from me, taking her hand as we passed in the figure, being the recipient of her smiles —yes, this was a pleasure indeed. I could think of few which might be greater, and all involving her.

How I regretted not dancing with her the night we met! This delight would not be new to me, had I behaved better then. I might even have had the right to call her 'Elizabeth' in more than my thoughts. But she smiled at me again as we clasped hands and crossed, and I gave up all thought of remorse and revelled in the joy that was presently mine.

I danced the next with Miss Bennet, Bingley and Elizabeth taking the places next to us, leaving me not entirely bereft of her company. Farther down the line, Miss Bingley danced as ostentatiously as she did everything else, drawing attention to the fact that she was partnered by a baronet. For all that he was twice her age, they made a fine pair, for Sir Walter Elliot is at least as conceited as she. But perhaps I am the wrong person to judge anyone for that failing.

During the third, Bingley and Elizabeth and I were engaged in a friendly conversation about music, though most of Bingley's attention was reserved for Miss Bennet as she moved through the dance with another gentleman. This suited me perfectly well, for it allowed me to focus upon Elizabeth without being rude. Fortunately, Miss Bingley also had a partner for the set, though she would follow me about the room for the next two.

At last the supper set arrived and I shook off my befeathered barnacle to claim Elizabeth's hand once more. Our second set was even more delightful than the first, for we had got over that little awkwardness of dancing together for the first time after all that had passed between us on that subject, and were free to simply enjoy ourselves. We spoke, when the dance allowed, of the country, and I did my best to tempt her with descriptions of the best paths at my estate. As little as I would wish to be accepted only for my property, I was not above using it, or anything else, to draw her affections.

We sat with Bingley and Miss Bennet for the meal, and there I found that Bingley's lady, albeit reticent, spoke sense when she chose to speak at all. For my friend's sake, I was glad to know that she had more than beauty and kindness to recommend her, though the latter is no small thing. It would be no hardship to be closely connected to her, should I be so fortunate as to win Elizabeth's hand—a notion which her smiles and laughter suggested was not impossible.

None of us had a partner for the set immediately following the meal, and we were happy to continue together rather than find other amusements. Miss Bingley soon joined us, and I was required to develop a sudden thirst and depart for the refreshments table to prevent her from claiming my arm uninvited. When I returned, she was speaking to Elizabeth, while Bingley and Miss Bennet looked on in obvious discomfort.

CHAPTER 25

ELIZABETH BENNET

"I hope, Miss Eliza, you will not allow Mr Darcy's attentions this evening to turn your head. I would hate to see you disappointed again. As your uncle has become such a great friend of his, he must do his part to return you to the acceptance of society, though I am unsure if even Mr Darcy's consequence is up to that task."

So involved was she in venting her spleen that she did not notice the gentleman's approach from her left until he addressed her.

"Miss Bingley, cease," he said sternly. "Your attempts to belittle Miss Elizabeth reflect poorly only on you." She gaped at him for a moment before subsiding into wounded silence. Meanwhile, I was wrestling with an epiphany. This man, this kind, haughty, charming, taciturn, protective, confounding man, was one I could love, and perhaps already did.

Flustered, I excused myself and repaired to the ladies' retiring room, where I thankfully found no one I knew. I placed myself by the window, which had been opened an inch for the relief of those who became overheated in the dance, and allowed the cold air to soothe my burning face.

Was there ever a creature more ridiculous than I? That I should by turns have opened my heart to a scoundrel and to a man I had despised for much of our acquaintance was a greater farce than I would have expected to find in the pages of a novel, much less my own life! Jane soon came to find me, and I feigned composure. She thought I had been overset by Miss Bingley's claims, and I told only a little untruth when I said that though I did not believe her words, it had been rather mortifying to have her suppositions voiced in the middle of a ballroom. This I would repeat to Mr Darcy, who approached us with concern writ large upon his face when we returned. A new set was forming, and when my sister's partner claimed her, I allowed him to escort me to my aunt before I urged him to do his duty by Lady Matlock and dance with one of her guests.

I cannot say that I liked seeing him dance with another, but he did not seem to be enjoying himself as he had with me, and I took a certain shameful comfort in that. Viscount Deane asked me for the last, and as Mr Darcy's aunt had just introduced him to a young lady, he too was in the set, and we were close enough that we passed each other several times and even exchanged a few words. As he returned me to my aunt and uncle, the viscount surprised me by commenting that Lady Deane had been 'wild' to meet me since hearing of my refusal to dance with Mr Darcy some weeks previous. "But now, I think, all is mended between you?"

I was happy to answer that it was.

We expected no callers the day after the ball, and were surprised when Mr Darcy arrived. I noticed immediately that he was rather resplendent: his hair freshly trimmed, his waistcoat a pleasant green embroidered in cream, unlike the more sombre hues he favoured, a jewelled pin twinkling amid the folds of his cravat. When my aunt offered him refreshment, he said, "I had hoped that Miss Elizabeth would care to take a walk in your garden, madam. The sun is out, and it is not so chill as yesterday."

I answered that I should enjoy a walk very much, if Jane would attend us. My sister smiled—was there something a little sly in it?—and said, "I fear it will be too cold for me, though I know you will walk in any weather, Lizzy. But I should be happy to sit by the window in the rear parlour, where I can see the whole of the garden."

My aunt was amenable to this plan, and sent me off to don my warmest pelisse, bonnet, and gloves. Mr Darcy's attire had raised a suspicion in my mind, and the rather permissive behaviour of my relations, coupled with the open pleasure he had taken in my sister's suggestion, firmed it into a near certainty. By the time we stepped out into the crisp January sunshine, my heart was pounding in my ears.

Before I could say anything at all, Mr Darcy laid his hand over mine, where it rested on his arm, and said,

"There is something very important I should like to say to you, if you are willing to hear me."

"Oh, let us not be hasty!" I cried. "I have allowed my feelings to run away with me before, to my detriment." It was not until a satisfied smile crept across his face that I realised I had given myself away.

"So you do care for me," he said softly. "Tell me, then, why you hesitate."

I found myself unable to meet his tender gaze. I resolutely faced forward and pretended a great interest in the browned remains of the summer's greenery. "I have told you a little of my family," I began, feeling that there was no point in dancing about the main reason for my reluctance. "They can be quite ill-behaved. I think you ought to meet them before anything irrevocable passes between us, sir. You might very well think better of our association, having done so, and I would not engage your honour only to embroil us both in a lifetime of regret."

He was silent for a long moment, though his hand tightened upon mine. "I have," he said at last, "any number of unpleasant acquaintances I must maintain, if only for my uncle's sake and my sister's acceptance in society when she comes out. I also have mentioned, I think, an aunt in Kent who is nothing less than a harridan. I had assumed that if you were willing to tie your life to mine, you would bear the trials of these associations for my sake. Can you not believe that I would be willing to do the same for you?"

He stopped, and placed himself before me, availing himself of both of my hands. "Dearest, loveliest Elizabeth. I know I have not always shown patience with that which I cannot like, but I swear to you that I have learnt my lesson. You need never fear that my behaviour will mortify you in future, or that the actions of anyone else could affect my regard for you. Say that you will marry me, my love, and together we will face all the follies of the world and laugh at them."

I am indeed a ridiculous creature, but not fool enough to disbelieve such an earnest entreaty from the best man I know. I smiled at him, and his anxious expression shifted to one of hope when I said, "Together. I like the sound of that."

"Then you will?"

"Yes, I will marry you, and we will brave your unfortunate connexions and mine, and be happy despite them."

"We shall be happy, Elizabeth. I will not allow anything else." His low declaration, almost a whisper, sent a shiver up my spine, which became a tremor of delight throughout my entire form as his lips claimed mine.

Oh, yes. We would be happy. There could not be two opinions on that point.

The End

ACKNOWLEDGMENTS

I'd like to thank the Quills and Quartos team, who invited me to step into the previously unexplored territory of writing a novella, and polished the result to a high shine.

To the family members and friends who said "you can do it" long before I submitted my first manuscript and were still honestly excited when this, my third, was accepted for publication: thank you for your unwavering support. You are the reason I keep going even when I feel like I'm writing pure rubbish.

And last but not least, my heartfelt appreciation to everyone who chose to spend their time with the fancies and follies contained in these pages. I hope they gave you joy.

ABOUT THE AUTHOR

Frances Reynolds fell madly in love with *Doctor Who* at the tender age of seven. This, in turn, led her to embrace other quintessentially British delights such as tea, scones, Dickens, and Austen. When she is not wrangling wild data for a large financial firm, she is generally to be found reading, writing, or watching her favorite series (*see above*) while knitting.

Frances lives slightly south of Canada with her spouse and a small herd of cats, in a house which is continually upset that it has been obliged to remain standing since 1916.

ALSO BY FRANCES REYNOLDS

In Sickness & In Health

It was not long before she honestly felt that she could love him, if he truly wished it.

When a smallpox epidemic sweeps through Hertfordshire, Elizabeth Bennet finds herself trapped together at Netherfield Park with Mr Darcy. An epidemic plagues Meryton and Longbourn village and Elizabeth and Darcy, unexpectedly immune, must work together to help those afflicted. Elizabeth finds herself forced to reconsider the character of the man she had deemed proud and disagreeable in light of his efforts.

Fitzwilliam Darcy is immune smallpox but finds himself all too susceptible to the charms of Elizabeth Bennet. First drawn to her as merely a friend, his feelings deepen as he witnesses her care for her family and neighbours as they face death, sorrow, and the ravages of the disease.

When the immediate peril subsides, a new threat arises in the form of damaging rumours spread in London. Darcy finds that he must determine whether his feelings for Elizabeth can override his more practical objections while Elizabeth must decide whether her grieving family's needs outweigh her own wishes. Can such connexions forged amid the fire of loss and adversity be made into a happily ever after?

In Sickness & in Health is a romantic variation of Jane Austen's Pride and Prejudice.

More Than a Pretty Face

It is a truth universally acknowledged that Elizabeth Bennet is the wittiest lady in Hertfordshire, and her sister Jane is the most beautiful. Their other qualities, however, are less widely recognised, even by those who profess to love them.

Disappointed by Mr Bingley's sudden departure, Jane escapes the tumult of Longbourn for the Gardiners' house in London. Elizabeth, vexed by her own romantic debacle with Mr Darcy, and in possession of distressing intelligence which could endanger their family and neighbours in Meryton, soon joins her there from Kent.

When a family crisis causes them to extend their stay in Cheapside, a new acquaintance—handsome and titled—brings the Bennet sisters to the attention of London society and returns them to the company of Mr Darcy and Mr Bingley. One man finds himself with a rival for his lady's affections, while the other struggles to make amends for the mistakes of the past.

As Elizabeth questions her rejection of the master of Pemberley and Jane begins to open her heart, can the qualities that most matter—intelligence, integrity, humour and kindness —be recognised by the men who truly love and respect them?

Made in the USA
Middletown, DE
13 August 2023

36605436R00090